MW01248726

IT WILL NEVER BE THE SAME.

PAULA AVILA

Paula Avila

Copyright © 2012 Author Name

All rights reserved.

ISBN-13:9798558416442

DEDICATION

We are handling one of the worst times of our lives because of COVID-19.

So many people are tragically dying because of this virus, and so many others are working to save lives.

My dedication and appreciation are for those incredible professionals that are there for us.

Their bravery will always be remembered by us.

Thank you for your sacrifice: doctors, nurses, first responders, teachers, firefighters, officers and so many other workers that are helping fight COVID-19.

1 John 1:9 – If we confess our **sins**, he is faithful and just to **forgive** us our **sins** and to cleanse us from all unrighteousness.

Psalm 103:10-14 – He has not punished us as we deserve for all our **sins**, for his mercy toward those who fear and honor him is as great as the height of the heavens above the earth.

PERSONAL MESSAGE

In this book, and all other books that I wrote, I want women to understand that my main vision is always: women's thoughts and feelings as mother and wife.

One, because we, as mothers, can comprehend true love.

Two, because we, as a wife, have the feeling that we need to take care of our home, kids, and husband. Most of the time, we forget about ourselves in this life.

In my books, I play the game where a woman can make mistakes about their thoughts and feelings and start her life over again.
I hope you can enjoy this book and have time to enjoy yourself.

Paula Avila.

Paula Avila

ACKNOWLEDGMENTS

First and foremost, praises and thanks to the Lord, the Almighty, for his showers of blessings throughout my research work to complete this book.

Because most of the time, I come home, after working in my business for eight hours straight, and God always gives me the **ability** and motivation to keep writing. To give my best to others.

I would also like to thank my husband and my children for the patience, their love and continuing support to complete this book.

Thanks to Evan Mason, my friend from Colorado, who helped describe the beauty of the State.

1 CHAPTER

Rollins Pass, Colorado. The memories I had of this place when my family and I used to come here are truly endless. Ever since I could remember, my family and I would go on almost weekly trips up here and spend hours and hours just living in the outdoors. Nothing on this earth beats the smell of the grass as you walk on it, jumping into the cold lake after hours of the sun cooking your skin to a fine crisp, ending the day off telling stories around a poorly made campfire by a father who claims that he used to be a boy-scout, and stargazing into the dark, empty, endless sky until you slowly doze off to sleep. What I have just described to you was my entire childhood. I couldn't ask for anything more. That is how I began my life in Colorado, and I believe it would be a good way to end it too.

I find a nice rock to sit on and take a rest from our hike. The early morning breeze blows on my face as I already know I'm going to absolutely miss this place. As Cody finishes tying his shoe, I can't help but notice how much Valerie is surveying her surrounding area. She's really drawn to the mountain tops, but I can't seem to know why. Maybe the stark contrast of the brown rock and the blue atmosphere has caught her attention. Maybe it's the gargantuan size of the sleeping giants that bewilder her. Whatever it may be, it brings a smile to my face. It reminds me of when I was a kid like her. And it also makes me think that maybe, just maybe, that when my daughter puts down that phone of hers and doesn't constantly complain about the slow internet; she might actually have a brain in there and might actually enjoy something that isn't Snapchat. Or she could just be bored out of her mind without her beloved device. There is no internet out here after all. My other child Cody, I know is having a blast. He always does. Always the front of the pack when we go out, always the first to point out a specific animal we encounter, and as always, always the first one to get hurt. It's almost tradition. 3 years ago he chipped his tooth going off a rope swing, 2 years ago he sprained his wrists after tripping on a rock, and last year he broke his foot by trying to show Valerie how to land by rolling off of a high jump. I can only hope the increase in severity isn't a trend going into this year. Travis has already given him a rundown that he needs to be safe this time. My husband already has enough on his plate to deal with another broken bone.

I get off of my rock and we head off to find our next and last campground. We follow a small trail that breaks away from the main path and we find a nice patch of flat land. The trees surrounding our campsite provides a great deal of shade to our new home that we'll live in for the next few hours. We begin to set up camp; Cody and Valerie set up the little stove we brought while Travis and I deal with the tents.

"Lori, today really is stunning isn't it?" Travis asks me.

"Perfect Travis, Today is perfect". We smile at each other. I can tell he's really happy and so am I.

"Can you come here and help me with this, I never know how to do it". He waves his hand signaling for me to go to him. "So, are you ready to move to Connecticut?"

Connecticut. The Constitution State. I honestly do not know much about Connecticut besides the fact that it just seems like New York's and Massachusetts' little brother. But Travis got a phenomenal job offer there that we just could not refuse. Before we jumped to any decisions, we ran it by Cody and Valerie first. They were hesitant at first. I mean, I doubt they could point to Connecticut on a map if they were asked to, but they are excited for the change. The new school, culture, everything. Cody claims he will be able to "crush the new kid role" and "Get the starting quarterback spot on the first day of tryouts". You must admire the confidence. While Valerie just hopes the boys there are not ugly. And if they were able to see the salary Travis would be getting there is no chance, they'd turn it down either. So, we decided that we were indeed moving. Today is our last day in Colorado, and tomorrow morning we leave.

"I'm as ready as I can be". As the days have got closer and closer to moving day the butterflies in my stomach have only got stronger and more rampant. I think Travis can see the nervousness in my face.

"Lori, it'll be fine. I agree, it will be scary at first but it's going to be an amazing experience. Trust me. The kids will love it there and so will you".

"I sure hope so". He still sees the nervousness.

He whispers a little "oh, come here" and ushers my lips to his, we kiss and he gives me a firm hug afterwards. We have been married for nineteen years and I still do not understand how he does it. We have never had any problems before and he treats me so well. I swear I live in a constant state of paradise with him.

.

2 CHAPTER

Cody manages to find a rope swing next to a lake and he and Valerie take turns doing flips off of it. You can hear the echoes of their laughter exponentially grow as they fall further and further down into the abyss. While Travis and I on the other hand take a seat on a nearby rock, shaded by 2 trees adjacent to the left of it, and admire the view. A few steps in front of us is the drop into the lake, which is a good 30 feet. Looking to the left there's a gravel trail circling around the lake, slowly declining onto a bank on the opposite side of the lake from us. Look to the right, there's a mountain. Travis also manages to spot 2 swans swimming next to each other. Swimming is a bit of an over exaggeration more, they're drifting along together, letting the water just push them along, without the slightest bit of worry. It was a peaceful sight; they really are such beautiful creatures and they look so good together. The laughter of your children, the view, your husband right next to you, you simply cannot put a price on moments like these. I pray Connecticut can deliver on giving us family time like this.

"You really had to go and burn my

marshmallow, not once, not twice, but for a third time?"

"It's not my fault you're scared of the fire"

"Well you have to at least try and make a good S'more. This isn't even a s'more anymore, it's crackers with chocolate topped with some burnt. That's it, just burnt."

"Why can't you just make your own Val?"

"Cody you know I'm not going near that thing!". Valerie is scared of fire, so she has Cody make her S'mores for her. I would say it would be nice of him, if he actually tried, and didn't burn the marshmallow into a slab of black burtness every time. So, it's almost becoming a yearly tradition that Cody burns her marshmallow a few times, until she complains, we tease her about us having good s'mores and she is in a grump for the rest of the night. But this year I didn't want her to have her final night in Colorado to be in a grump, so I gave her my s'more. I swear the way she ate that thing, I'm almost certain that she never ate a real s'more in her entire life.

"Connecticut huh?". Travis nudges me with his elbow. "How are the butterflies in that belly of yours" and he starts to jokingly poke me in the stomach and I laugh. I slap his hands away.

"They've been getting better; they've been getting better. I've come to terms that we are indeed going to leave this. Paradise". I give off a little sigh.

"Oh, stop it," he laughs and pushes me in my shoulder, "Connecticut is going to be paradise too. You have nothing to worry about, when it's us we can fly to the moon". He gently grabs my face and gives me a kiss. I smile.

We stay outside for a bit longer until the bugs just get too much to handle and we get up to go to our tents.

"Mom. I'm going to miss this place" I hear Valerie's light voice say. I pause for a little bit until I answer.

"Me too Val, me too Val."

.

3 CHAPTER

The sun is shining but the morning is calm. We wake up early as we agree to return home.

With everything in the car, we begin our departure. The children sleep in the car as we head home with broken hearts. I am having a hard time accepting the fact that we can no longer call Colorado our home.

But life needs to go on.

Travis is a scientist working in a large research lab here in Colorado. However, this excellent job offer from a major Connecticut college change everything. Travis believes that this new job opportunity could open the door for new research he intends to pursue.

We decided not to sell our mountain-top home as we can use it to ski during the winter months.

We stopped at a gas station on the way home to go to the bathroom and get something to eat. I know when I get to Connecticut, I'll need to focus on the moving in process.

We have already hired the company to move our furniture and cars. We will travel by plane and stay in a hotel until our new house is organized. The college has graciously paid for this process.

The children each got something to eat and I just wanted a coffee.

"Mom, can we throw a departure party with my friends?

"Wow, Valerie! We're too rushed and busy to think about partying, my daughter."

"Please, mom. I'll never see them again."

"Valerie, stop all this drama. Of course, you'll see them on vacation. Don't forget your grandmother lives in Colorado."

My mother is suffering a lot because our move to Connecticut, mainly because of the children. Although my father understands all this the most, he does not make his suffering apparent.

Travis' parents are also incredibly sad. However, they know that for Travis this opportunity is unique and Travis will be happier.

It's been a little tricky for everyone, but it is what is best for us.

When we got home, Travis went to the lab to finalize issues necessary for his departure. I stayed home organizing camp errands and checking the last details of the move. The kids went to visit their friends.

My mom calls me asking if we want to have dinner with them and I agree. I believe they want to be as close as possible to the kids. Soon, all this will change.

I spent a couple of hours on phone calls finalizing the rent of the house and last-minute documents. A rush of excitement fills my body.

Travis arrived shortly after finishing at the company and I told him we were having dinner at my mother's house. He nodded positively with his head and went to his office to finish organizing his books. Tomorrow morning, the moving truck will arrive.

"Travis? Baby?"

"Yes, Lori!"

"I'm going to run ok. When the kids arrive, ask

them to take a shower so we can have dinner at mama's house ok?"

"Sure, my love. Do we have more cardboard boxes?"

"Yes, we do Travis. They're inside our bedroom closed."

"Thank you, honey."

"You're welcome."

I put on my AirPods and went running. Nothing makes me feel calmer and happier than when running. Running relieves my stress and I always feel in a better mood.

We live in the Northern part of Boulder. It is a beautiful and very peaceful place.

I greeted some neighbors who wanted to hear about our trip to Connecticut, but I picked up speed so I did not have to explain myself.

4 CHAPTER

My mother prepared a beautiful dinner. It was a farewell dinner. My mother was shocked as she did not believe we would move away that far, but life is full of surprises.

Travis is super excited and happy. The job is excellent and the opportunity for himself to invest in his own research is a unique opportunity.

It was then at dinner, that Travis announced the day of our departure to Connecticut.

"Yes, folks. We will go this Friday."

"Really, Travis? Wow..." I was a little scared because I didn't know.

"Yeah, I need to be there on Friday afternoon."

"Oh no, darling! I will suffer too much." My mother mumbled and began to cry.

"Mom, the kids will come on vacation here. And you and daddy can go there anytime you guys want."

"I know daughter, but knowing you are far away hurt"

And for the rest of the night, we spoke about the new changes coming into our lives.

We left mama's house and went home. When I got there, I looked all around: everything packed, the house a little messy, but it was time to say goodbye.

Knowing the departure date made me a little uncomfortable. A little insecure perhaps.

Travis came and hugged me and said lovingly:

"Baby, it is time ... are you happy?"

"Travis, I am still unsure about this change. But I'm excited."

"Great, my love! I'm feeling the same. And thanks for embarking on this journey with me."

"Of course, Travis!"

I finalized putting our home decor in boxes since the moving truck will be here early tomorrow.

Travis went to his office to pack up his books. After a lot of work, everything was ready to go.

When we went to bed, it was extremely late. Travis looked tired and I probably did as well.

The moving truck arrived around seven in the morning. I was already awake for my morning run.

Our furniture was already organized so by noon, the moving truck was already on the road. Our house was completely empty.

The sight of the empty house reminded me of when Travis and I got married and moved here. It took us almost two months to get everything ready. Great memories!

Valerie and Cody began to feel the sadness of leaving. The empty house, friends coming to say goodbye, and packing, all made them sad. Valerie began to cry while Cody was just quiet.

Travis and I hugged them and comforted them. We, as adults, have more maturity for all this. On the other hand, they are just children suffering from the changes that life brings us.

Friday has arrived and it is the day of our departure. Friends and family came to the airport to say their goodbyes to us. My mother was very sad.

To my surprise, the children had smiles on their faces.

With all the stress of arranging the trip, a sudden surge of emotion came to me. My heart felt pain and a sudden urge not to go. Being around all my family and friends brought tears to my eyes.

We board onto the plane and it is time:

Here we go!

5 CHAPTER

We landed at Bradley Airport in Connecticut's capital, Hartford.

The kids and I never visited Connecticut. Travis came to visit the new job a couple of months ago so he knows the area a bit more. I am anxious but happy. I have butterflies in my stomach. I literally look like a teenager confronting the unknown. Not knowing what will be ahead, I have thousands of thoughts in my head and I am hoping for the best.

We rented a car at the same airport and went to our hotel in New Haven, CT.

Wow, what traffic! We were stuck in traffic for almost an hour. We were tired and wanted to arrive soon to rest. While we were stuck in traffic, we enjoyed the landscape of Connecticut: lots of trees, lots of trees indeed!

How beautiful! When we looked at trees nearby, there were deer eating. Valerie thought it was great to see the animals near the road, eating quietly.

"Mom, I think these deer are welcome to Connecticut."

"I think so, baby!"

We got into downtown New Haven and faced more traffic!

There were a lot of people on the street, a lot of movement. There were Yale Facilities everywhere. We arrived at the hotel and soon the reception came. Lots of bags.

We got out of the car and went to check-in. We were tired and needed a bath following a good dinner. I sat on the hotel reception sofa while Travis finished checking in. I think the thrill of this change and jetlag has exhausted me right now.

We head to our hotel room. Beautiful, large room, very elegant, and comfortable.

We decided to get room service. After cleaning up, we decided we wanted to just stay in and relax with pajamas.

While waiting for dinner, Travis worked on the computer and I was organizing our things. Cody and Valerie were almost dozing in bed.

When dinner came, happiness seems to have hit our souls ... we were very hungry. The children jumped out of bed. The hotel attendant came into the room with dinner and I set the table.

Over dinner, I looked at each of them, pondering what their plans would be for the next few months ahead.

Travis is very quiet. I already know that he is looking forward to new work and new projects.

"Travis, are you going to work tomorrow?"

"Yes, baby, I will. But only in the morning. In the afternoon I would like to see the houses that are available to us."

"Sure!"

"We have to decide which school district we would like the kids to attend.

"Dad, can I see your new office?"

"Sure Cody. You two can come."

Conversations like this made up our dinner: making plans and more plans. We finished dinner, organized the dishes, had the children brush their teeth, and we headed to bed.

I sat there on the couch waiting for Travis, who was extremely focused on his work. After an hour of waiting there, I decided to go to sleep. I was tired and did not want to disturb Travis.

6 CHAPTER

I didn't even see if Travis slept or not, I just saw him leaving early when he kissed me and said:

"See you later, baby."

I just opened my eyes and couldn't even respond. I gave a slight smile to him as he was leaving quickly.

I and the kids woke up around ten o'clock in the morning. I freaked out that we might be late to see the houses.

We got dressed and went to have coffee in the restaurant of the hotel. What a wonderful breakfast it was! We were delighted at that banquet. I stood watching the Connecticut view from above. A beautiful city and the sea is there embellishing our vision. Lots of trees; all very beautiful. The move from Colorado to here will hopefully be a very good experience for our children.

I am starting to enjoy all the new experiences.

Travis sent me a text message saying he has three houses for us to check out today.

Each house in ruling cities, but all around New Haven: Woodbridge, Orange, and a slightly further house in Guilford.

After breakfast, the kids and I went for a walk in downtown New Haven.

We went to the green and walked around Yale. We visited a modern art museum which was a great tour. We were shown the Peabody Museum which is an archaeology museum. The kids loved to see the dinosaur skeletons.

Travis calls me to say he will be back at the hotel around two o'clock.

Travis was very excited about his future. He talked about several projects planned within the university. He is finally achieving his dream of being the head coordinator of his own research team.

When Travis picked us up to house hunt, the car was filled with excitement. Valerie and Cody wanted to tell their dad about the adventures of the day while Travis was ecstatic to tell us about his day's work.

So, we follow our path to decide which house we will live in.

First, we went to Orange. A beautiful city. I love to see so many trees, so much nature. The houses are beautiful. We arrived at the house in Orange.

It was a stunning house but I did not like the garden. The house was amazing, but I could not see myself living there. The school district was very good, but I wanted to see the other home options we have.

Following that, we went to Woodbridge. Loved the house. Everything was perfect for me and the school was great too. The children were delighted with the houses. They didn't know what they wanted. Travis was happy to see our joy in deciding which house to choose.

"Travis, I think this is our house. I love the idea of living in a cul-de-sac. This street is so quiet and has a lot of nature around it."

"I liked it a lot too, Lori. Anyway, I find it interesting to visit Guilford's house."

"Of course, we will."

Heading to Guilford, we saw a lot of nature, but the traffic was more intense. Travis mentioned his concerns of taking this commute with much traffic.

"Lori, I think Guilford is far away. I'll have to spend a lot of time in traffic. This time, which could be with you."

"I agree with you, Travis."

"But let's go into it with an open mind."

We were delighted with the city of Guilford. So much tranquility. All very beautiful and near the sea. The house was older but cozy.

We went back to the hotel and talked about what would be the best option for us to live. I liked Woodbridge very much, but Travis didn't mention his wants, nor the kids.

Arriving back in New Haven, we had dinner at a fish restaurant. We sat outside the restaurant and enjoyed the sea that was leaning against the restaurant.

"So, guys? What house?" Travis asked.

"I liked the house in Orange, but whatever for me, dad," Cody replied.

"I liked Guilford's, but I already know it's far away, Dad. So, I vote for the Woodbridge house." Valeria gave her input.

"I vote for the house in Woodbridge." I said.

"I liked the Woodbridge house. It's a big, very comfortable house. When our parents come to visit us there's room for them to stay." Travis spoke with a great argument.

So, the waitress brought me and Travis wine and juice for the kids. And we celebrate our new life in Connecticut. Our new home!

7 CHAPTER

As soon as Travis left for work, I got up to organize our lives. The moving truck will arrive in a couple of days. All that is missing is giving the deposit to the landlord.

I called a cleaning company and got them to clean the house, especially the kitchen and bathrooms.

My mother texted me a message asking how we were doing. I talked to her about the new house and that everything was going well.

After the house was decided, I called the school in the city and made an appointment to visit the school.

Cody and Valerie woke up already making plans with the new school and house in mind. I smiled and let them talk. I then asked them to get organized so we could get breakfast.

Travis texted me a message saying he was going to get the house key tomorrow.

Wow, everything seems to be going as planned.

After breakfast, I left the kids in the hotel pool and went back to the rooms to organize our clothes. I went downstairs to do some laundry.

That same day, Travis came late from work. The kids and I stayed at the hotel all day. Cody and Valeria stayed in the pool all day while I spent my time at the gym. I ran, worked out, and did Zumba. A group of dancers were there at the gym and I asked if I wanted to join them.

At about four o'clock in the afternoon, the kids and I showered and waited for Travis.

I was on my laptop giving a last glance at my calendar to see what is upcoming: move into home, children's school and organizing the furniture.

Connecticut seems to have welcomed us very well, I think! Everything seems to be fitting perfectly.

"Mom, what time is Dad coming? I'm hungry."

"Calm down Cody! He's coming soon."

I'd rather send a message to Travis to find out if he's coming soon or not. I don't like to bother Travis when he's working. He gets very focused and doesn't like to be disturbed.

"Stuck in traffic!"

Travis answered quickly. He said he will arrive in about 20 minutes.

To distract the boys, I asked them to pack their belongings because in two days, we would move into a new home. Valerie got up and packed her things while Cody complained that he was hungry.

When the hotel room door opened, I was so happy knowing Travis was there. It seems that this change of State, Colorado to Connecticut, has brought us all closer together.

Both the kids and I went towards Travis and hugged him tightly.

"Dad, we miss you! You arrived late today, why?"

"I was working, Valerie."

"How was your day baby with them?"

"It was great, Travis. Today was a day of pool and gym."

"That's great then! Let's have dinner?"

"Please, I'm starving ..." Cody begs.

"I know, I know Cody, so let's go."

I grabbed my bag and we went to dinner. Travis barely had any time to rest before we left.

We went to a great Italian restaurant in downtown New Haven. We had a great family night and a great dinner.

Returning to the hotel, the kids went to sleep while I talked to Travis, who was in the shower.

During our conversation, I noticed such enthusiasm at Travis. He had a thousand plans. The college was giving great support to him and his projects. It had been a while since I had seen my husband so happy. It's great to see you like that. :)

8 CHAPTER

The next morning, we woke up early. Travis went to work while the kids and I went to our new home.

As soon as we got to the house in Woodbridge, the cleaning company was waiting for us. I ran to give them instructions on cleaning the bathrooms and kitchen.

I started vacuuming as the kids swept the deck. The moving truck was scheduled to arrive around two o'clock in the afternoon. Looks like everything was on time.

At around twelve o'clock I ordered pizza for everybody at the house: me, the kids, and the cleaning staff. Wow, we were very hungry. We ended up eating three large pizzas.

Travis texted me asking me if all was well, and I said yes. He said he would be at the new house at around four in the afternoon to help us.

The moving truck arrived and the busyness all started: Slowly but surely, everything was falling into place.

The moving company employees were very professional and everything was very well organized. What a delight it was to organize our new home.

After all of the furniture was in the house, I stayed in the kitchen arranging pots, plates, and glasses while the children, each in their own room, kept organizing their clothes and decorations. I'm very happy to see Cody and Valerie with such enthusiasm.

Around four in the afternoon, Travis arrived with some snacks for us. He was shocked by how clean and organized everything was.

"Wow, my love! Does everything seem to be ready? What beauty!"

"Almost. It took a bit of work but it was faster than I imagined!"

"Daddy, come to see my room!" shouted Valeria from her room.

Travis went to look at the rooms of the house and the children's bedrooms. I continued unwrapping the cups and plates in the kitchen!

"Our love, great work! Everything is fine."

"It was all so easy because the moving company people were so efficient."

"How can I help Lori?"

"Travis, can you please put the cups in that cabinet and the plates in that middle cabinet over there."

We continued to talk and organize in the kitchen.

"Travis, I think we will be ready to move in tomorrow."

"Oh really?"

"Yes, definitely. Tomorrow we can leave the hotel, leave the kids here and go shopping at the supermarket."

"Great Lori! Nothing better than our house."

"How was your work today, Travis?"

"Everything is great! I've already put projects in motion. I've selected some students to help develop this. Next week, I'll present my research studies to the whole team."

"Wow! Congratulations Travis!"

With everything almost ready, we went back to the hotel.

"Early tomorrow we will move to the new home." I told the kids.

When I said that, the children jumped with joy.

I was exhausted. Moving and organizing all

day got the best of me.

9 CHAPTER

Well, a week into the new house, everything seems to be in order. I bought everything I needed and our house looks beautiful!

Last week, we finally decided on a school for the kids. All the pieces are starting to fit together! School will start next week. We have been going out buying supplies so they could succeed in their classes.

I go on a run every morning. Our house is located in a well-wooded area that has many running trails.

The smell of the trees gives me a sense of calmness. Energy and the feeling of accomplishment hit my body when I finish. I still miss Colorado's landscape but Connecticut is still beautiful.

Right after my run, I arrange breakfast for my loving family.

Travis is living a dream in his professional career. Everything is going very well for him and I could not be more excited to see him succeed.

I wonder what I will do to take up my time when the kids go back to school. I have not painted much since attending art school so I am hoping to start back up again.

Upon arriving home after my run, I noticed that my neighbor was waiting for me.

"Hi, my name is Laura! I'm your next-door neighbor."

"Hi, I'm Lori."

"Welcome, Lori! I brought banana bread to your family."

"Wow, thank you so much, Laura."

"Do you like running?"

"Yeah, I like to run in the morning."

"I hope you like banana bread, Lori. I'm going to work and we'll talk to you soon. If you need anything, you know where to find me!"

"Thank you very much, Laura. We will definitely love the banana cake. See you."

Along with the banana bread came a welcome card with their telephone number and names. How cute is that!

I went inside and began making breakfast: milk, cereal, and banana bread. I took the opportunity to make a fresh coffee. Soon Travis went down to work.

"How was the morning running, baby?"

"It was great, Travis. Look what our neighbor brought us: banana bread."

"Delicious! I will try it out with my coffee."

"Very good banana bread. Baby, I need to go. Today I'll be back later from work, okay?"

"Are you coming for dinner?"

"I don't think so but save me a plate of food in the oven. When I get home, I will warm it up."

"Of course! I can do that."

We kissed and Travis went to work. I took advantage of the time the kids are still asleep to unpack some boxes in the basement.

The new house is a great feeling, but it is a lot of work to put everything in order.

Cody woke up, ate cereal and went to read a book while Valerie continued to sleep. I continued in the basement. The week consisted of preparing for school and organizing the house!

10 CHAPTER

The day started a bit later today so I will only be able to run after the kids go to their first day of school and Travis goes to work.

This weekend was great. We visited Manhattan, NY. We began our day with visiting the Statue of Liberty. We then rode rental bikes through Central Park. We finished the day having dinner at an amazing Brazilian Steakhouse in downtown Manhattan.

After dinner, we went to Times Square to see the glow of the city. It was beautiful!!! I love Manhattan.

Today, Cody and Valerie will embark on a great journey with their new school. I think they are excited to meet their new peers.

They ate cereal and went to school. Travis soon left for work. I went running...

As I ran, I kept pondering about how life changes without us even noticing. I never thought of living in another state. But here we are today, filled with different plans and new dreams!

Life comes and goes, but we must be prepared for the changes that come our way. Travis has been so excited to be progressing in his career and I am extremely happy that I get to help. I know my support is especially important to him and our children.

I am willing to give my family all the support they need to win.

Returning home from my jog, I ran into Laura again.

"Hi Lori, how are you?"

"Hi Laura, I'm fine and you?"

"I am well, thanks. Lori, my husband Chris, and I are going to host a little cookout. I was wondering if you and your family could come. It would be a great time to meet everyone."

"I think it's a great idea! I will call Travis and I will let you know what time we will be there."

"Perfect then! We'll be waiting."

"Thank you, Laura."

"It's a pleasure, Lori!"

Wow! I loved the invite from Laura. I'm in need of new friends. After the rush of organizing everything, relaxing with friends will be great for us. I called Travis and he also liked the invitation. I then texted Laura and told her we'd be at her house around six o'clock in the afternoon. She told me that was perfect.

I went to buy wine and flowers to bring for the cookout this evening.

I'm excited to go visit the new neighbors. It's great to feel welcomed and to feel that we are starting our move on the right foot.

11 CHAPTER

We arrived at our neighbor's house at about quarter past six.

We began getting introduced to many family members and friends. We were finally able to meet Laura's husband, Chris. They had two children: Luke, who was in his mid-twenties and Julia, who was eighteen.

A beautiful table with cold cuts and fruits was waiting for us. How elegant was their garden decor? Just perfect!

"Hi guys, how are you? Welcome, everyone!"

Laura's husband spoke.

"Thank you very much for the invitation. We feel really welcome!" Travis replied.

We all shook hands and soon followed the wine. Our first convening with the neighbors seemed to be going very well ... We felt a genuinely nice connection.

Travis and I explained our reasons for the move and all the emotions that came with it.

After a while, my kids went home while Travis and I stayed at the party.

I sat in the garden to enjoy the beauty. When I noticed Laura's eldest son,

Luke, he sat down next to me.

"How are you guys enjoying Connecticut, Lori?"

"We are really enjoying it."

"I already realized that you run every morning here on the street."

"Yes, I love to run. There, in Colorado, we played a lot of outdoor sports."

"I also run every day. I played basketball when I was in college! Sport is my passion."

"How cool, basketball? I played basketball in high school. Wow, what a good coincidence!"

"I think we'd better go over there, Luke."

"Sure, Lori! Can I run with you any of these days?"

I thought the question was strange, but I said yes trying not to be rude.

We went back to the party and stayed close

to Travis. I don't know why, but I was uncomfortable with my conversation with Laura's son, Luke. I thought he was a boy, but already a man. His charm really caught me by surprise.

I stopped thinking about what happened and went back to the conversation. What a great couple our neighbors made. They are lively and fun to talk to. They were excellent hosts.

Travis and I went home at around 10 at night. I was happy to see that Travis relaxed a little. All this change, the new job, and the new home brought tension. But it seems that he got his time off. We are incredibly happy.

When we got home, I realized that Travis and I were a bit drunk. I laughed because I rarely saw Travis drink.

We went upstairs and went to check on the children who were already asleep. They have to get up early for school tomorrow.

When we arrived at the room, I realized that Travis was trying to make love.

He was hot and saying things I like to hear before making love.

I turned and kissed him on the mouth. The kiss was delicious. It felt like we were young in a different place. Travis was all bold: he kissed and touched me like never before. He took off my clothes and looked at me with much desire and it turned me on. We made love and it was wonderful.

I enjoyed it and was filled with pleasure and warmth. I love to have sex with my husband.

12 CHAPTER

I got up around six in the morning and went to prepare breakfast. The children soon woke up and came to have coffee.

"Mom, it was nice yesterday at the neighbors' house, wasn't it?"

"Yes, it was, Valerie. It was incredibly good."

"I thought it was boring," Cody spoke.

"Wow, son, it was fine."

"For you adults! But for me, it was boring."

I smiled because that might have been true.

Travis then came down. He was looking very elegant.

"Wow, my husband is charming today! I'm going to be jealous, huh?"

We kissed. He made his coffee while I toasted him a piece of bread.

"Lori, honey, what's your plan for today?"

"Well, Travis, I'm going to run after cleaning the house and finishing some laundry. Why? Do you need me?"

Before Travis answered, the kids left the table to get ready for school.

"Yes, Lori, I need you to take these signed papers to the rental broker."

"Of course, I can, my love ... after last night I can do anything you want ..."

Travis and I smiled... we talked about last night with our new neighbors.

We agreed that it was a great first meeting with them.

Everyone is gone: kids for school and Travis for work.

I started organizing the kitchen, cleaning the bathrooms, and putting the laundry in. While the laundry was in, I decided to run. I put on my running shoes stretched.

When I left the house, I saw that someone from Laura's house was leaving on a motorcycle. I didn't pay much attention and started running.

I put on my AirPods, put on music, and started running while enjoying the nature around my street.

When I arrived at the street near mine, I

realized that something was approaching me ... it was the person on the motorcycle. I stopped running and looked to see who it was. The motorcycle also stopped and the person took off his helmet. It was Luke, my neighbor's son.

"Hey?" I was a little confused.

"Hi, Lori! How are you? Are you running?"

"Yes, running now because I need to leave later."

"Okay, enjoy it then. See you later."

And he was gone. Strange, but maybe he was just being kind and I'm going crazy.

Today is a beautiful day: A bright sun, a delicious wind and a pine scent that reminded me of Colorado.

Listening to this music and feeling that nature makes me feel so good.

It feels as if I am renewing myself physically and psychologically.

I love being alive to enjoy everything.

After running for two hours, I came home, organized things, and left to bring the documents that Travis asked me to bring.

13 CHAPTER

I arrived in downtown New Haven to take care of the documents that needed to be delivered. I took the opportunity to walk around downtown.

There are many stores, the green is beautiful, and I was fascinated by everything there. I sat in a coffee shop. I took a book and read it while sipping my coffee. I was actually killing time.

As I walked through the city of New Haven, I entered the Church in front of the green. It was a beautiful church that had fantastic architecture.

Travis texted and asked if I was still in New Haven, so I said yes.

He invited me to lunch with him because he had to go to the city later in the day.

I agreed and we met at a Brazilian steakhouse that was close to me. Wow, It was an incredible amount of food.

When we met, we kissed. Travis and I try to always be affectionate with each other, because we don't want the routine of our lives to cool our love.

"Hi baby, how is your day?"

"It's okay, Travis. And yours?"

"Very good so far. My mom called wanting to see the possibility of spending Thanksgiving together."

"Wow, that would be cool. Would we go to Colorado or would they come here?"

"We didn't go into that much detail, but we'll see."

"I think I would like to go to Colorado."

"But it would be nice if our parents got to know Connecticut."

"You're right, Travis. I think I miss Colorado a little."

"I understand you, Lori. I have been so busy lately that I barely have had any time to miss it.

"Maybe they'll come to Connecticut for Thanksgiving and we spend Christmas in Colorado? What do you think?"

"I think it's a great idea."

We were attended by a waitress who took us to a table and explained to us about the steakhouse and barbecue. After that, we went to enjoy the salad table. Shortly after, they brought the meat to our table.

Everything was incredibly good and tasty.

We finished our lunch. Travis went back to his work and I went home.

I got home and kept walking around. I'm getting tired of doing nothing ...

Soon, I will need to do something. Maybe I will send my resume to the city's school so I can possibly teach some art classes. I don't know, but I need to do something soon.

The kids arrived from school, had a snack, and went to their room.

I am alone all the time. I took advantage and called my mother. I commented with her about Thanksgiving and Christmas. She loved the idea and she said that she would like to know more about Connecticut.

Thanksgiving is a few months away, but maybe this event could take up more of my time. I'm already sure that I will need to buy more dishes and pans for Thanksgiving dinner. I will also come up with new ideas to accommodate everyone.

14 CHAPTER

Today, the day began with rain. I got up to prepare breakfast for my babies, but I wondered what time I would run. With this rain, it won't work.

When everyone left, I cleaned the house. When I looked outside, I saw that the rain stopped.

I changed my clothes and went running. The ground was wet and there were already some colorful leaves on the ground hinting that autumn is coming.

For a moment, I realized that the floor was slippery, but I kept running.

Travis texted me asking if I wanted to go out to dinner today. When I went to answer back, I got distracted and fell.

Wow, I don't remember falling for years ... and I think something happened to my foot: I broke my foot or twisted it. Come on, it hurts a lot. My hands were dirty from the wet floor and my cell phone flew away from me.

I stopped right there on the floor and tried to figure out what to do. My foot hurts so much!

When I looked up, I saw someone coming to help me. It was my neighbor's son Luke.

"Lori? Are you ok?"

"Hi, Luke! I fell and I think I twisted my foot."

"Wow, the floor is wet ..."

"Yes, I think so."

"I'll help you up."

Luke was a strong and muscular man. He picked me up as if I was nothing.

"Ah, oh my foot is hurting a lot. I don't think I can stand on the floor."

"Then you must have broken or twisted your foot."

"Luke, can you get my phone over there? It flew when I fell."

"I'll call Travis to come and get me."

"Call him later, Lori. I'll carry you home and I'll take you to the hospital. Anyway, he'll be here soon."

"No, I don't want to give you a hard time."

"That will be a pleasure. Come here ..."

And Luke carried me over to his house and we went to Yale. On the way to the hospital, I called Travis who started heading there.

After warning Travis, I calmed down a little. I thanked Luke for his help.

For a moment, after the shock, I accidentally looked at Luke and noticed his muscles, his strong arms and the charm there ... I was confused by looking at that boy who was helping me. He was so sexy that I had to change the direction of my eyes.

My heartbeat faster when I looked at him again.

He asked me:

"Are you better or is your foot still hurting, Lori?"

"It is hurting more than before, I think."

"We're almost at Yale's emergency room, okay?"

"Okay Luke, thank you very much."

When we arrived at the emergency room door, a wheelchair soon came. Luke took me in his arms and gently placed me in the chair.

"Lori, I'm going to park the car and soon I'll

meet you inside the hospital, ok?"

"Okay, Luke, thanks."

I hope that Travis arrives here at the hospital soon. They put me on a stretcher and went for an x-ray.

After finding the results, they put a boot on my foot. I didn't break my foot, but I twisted it.

I was exhausted with pain and so much delay.

Neither Luke nor Travis was with me during the journey inside the hospital.

After two hours or so, I went to a room until I was discharged from the doctor.

Then Travis came ...

"Hi, my love, are you better?"

and kissed me.

"Hi, Tavis, what an agony to stay here without seeing you. Wow, I thought I would have to live here ... Did you talk to the kids? Are they okay?"

"Yes Lori, they are fine. I ordered pizza for them because I didn't know what time we were going to get home."

"How nice Travis."

"Luke had to go to his house. It looks like he needed to do a job interview."

"Wow, Travis, this kid helped a lot. How cute."

"Yes, he was all worried. I thought he was even more worried than he should be."

"Ahahah ... I know Travis. He just wanted to help."

"Yes, it did help."

15 CHAPTER

After four long hours at the hospital, Travis and I went home.

We got home and the kids came running to see their "hurt" mother.

"Hi, guys! How are you?"

"Hi mom, how are you?"

"I'm fine guys. I'm just going to hobble for a few days."

"And now mom? You won't be able to run anymore, huh?" Cody asked. And that's when I realized this: I'm not going to run for a long time. This will bring me a lot of sadness.

"Yes, Cody, I won't be able to run."

Entering the house, the doorbell rang: it was

Laura and Luke.

"Hello Lori, are you feeling better?" Laura asked.

"Hi Laura, yes I am."

"I brought this banana cake for you to snack on later."

"Wow! You didn't have to bother Laura but thank you very much."

"No problem, Lori! Now if you need anything, I can help you, okay?"

"Thank you, Laura, and thank you, Luke, for today. You were an angel."

"It was a pleasure, Lori. I'm so sorry that you got hurt. You won't be able to run for a while."

"No, I won't be able to run ..."

We stayed talking for a while. I was really tired and my foot still hurt. But everyone wanted to comment on this event.

Luke and Laura left and the kids went to bed. I went to take a shower. Travis helped me take my shower and change clothes. My body just wanted a bed.

"Travis, my love. Tomorrow morning, I don't think I'm going to feel good enough to make breakfast for you and the kids."

"Don't worry, baby! I'm going to get up early to organize everything."

"I'm so sorry for the inconvenience. But this accident got me down."

"Lori, don't worry, everything will be fine. Soon, you'll be fine."

"I hope, Travis."

I took a sleeping pill and knocked out.

The next morning, when I woke up, everyone had already left. Travis left me a glass of water and the medicine I need to take.

My foot was still hurting when I tried to walk. I took my crutches and went to the bathroom to pee.

I thought it would be worse, but I can handle it.

I prepared my coffee and ate a piece of banana cake that Laura brought me last night.

Someone knocked on the door and I went to see who it was.

"Hi Luke, how are you?"

"I'm sorry to bother you, Lori, but I wanted to see if you're okay."

"Thanks, Luke, I'm fine."

I didn't even open the door because I was still in my pajamas.

"If you need me, call me. I mean, if you need help."

"Okay, Luke, thanks."

"This is my telephone number, call me anytime."

"Sure, I'll call."

I closed the door and remembered that our boxes for Thanksgiving arrived. Boxes that I bought from Amazon with tablecloths and napkins. I opened the back door and called Luke.

"Luke, I'm sorry, but there are two boxes in the garage. Do you think you can bring them to me?"

He turned quickly and smiled. That gorgeous smile. He looks more like a magazine model than my neighbor.

"Of course, Lori," Luke answered.

He came in. I closed the door and showed him where the boxes were.

Luke, with those strong arms, had no problem holding on. I asked him to put it in the kitchen. Now, I will have a lot of time to fix things at home. Without running or being able to go anywhere, I will unpack things for Thanksgiving.

"Luke, do you want some juice or water?"

"I think I will accept the water, Lori."

He took the glass and poured himself water.

"Is your foot hurting today, Lori?"

"A little. I took medicine, but it still hurts."

"When are you going back to the hospital?"

"Next week."

Luke and I had a connection the very first day we talked. I find him truly kind and he is always offering help. Even more, I like to be with him and look at his beauty.

Good thing Travis called me at that weird moment. Then I could come back to reality: what's going on with my head.

While talking to Travis, I realized that Luke was looking at me ... he was looking at my body and my hair. He turned his face away but kept looking again at my body. Those looks bothered me a little, but I liked it.

When he looked at me, I felt sexy.

What is happening to me?

I finished talking to Travis.

"So, okay, Luke. Thank you so much for your help."

"No problem Lori. Let me know if there is anything I could do to help."

"Thanks."

I went to bed for a little while, my foot is in a lot of pain.

16 CHAPTER

The kids came home from school and I was still in bed. Today was a bit more difficult for me to get up. I called the pizzeria and ordered pizza, salad, and bread.

I called Travis and told him that today I couldn't really do anything today. I explained how the house isn't organized and I couldn't even prepare dinner. As always, my husband was kind and said that when he arrives, he will organize everything.

I walk or put weight on my sprained foot as long as it does not hurt. It is almost impossible. My doctor gave me an immobilizer, I wore it as directed. I avoid hot showers, hot tubs, or hot packs. I called Travis to hopefully cheer me up...

"Baby, I could have made dinner. But pizza is great!!!"

"Thanks, Travis. I was worried about the kids."

"I will be home soon and don't worry about anything. When I arrive home, I will organize everything."

"Thanks, Travis ..."

On the first day, I was tired of not doing anything.

There is so much to do: Wash clothes, clean the kitchen… and clean the house. I asked the kids to clean the bathrooms and they did.

Before Travis arrived, Laura came to our house and brought roasted chicken. How cute is she? This neighbor of mine is an angel. Laura works all day and has time to help.

"Hi Laura, thanks for the roast chicken."

"That's fine, Lori, it is my pleasure. Do you feel better today?"

"Laura, I do not. I am in agony when I stand up."

"I understand, but it is better to rest for you

to recover quickly."

"Truth!"

"I saw that you ordered pizza, leave the chicken for tomorrow."

"When Travis arrives, he'll take care of that. It's hard to stay home like that, but what can I do, right? Thank you so much for your love, Laura."

"Don't worry, Lori ... Everything will be fine, don't stress."

Laure left and it got me thinking how many things we don't value. I was so happy and healthy. Now, a not so serious accident, makes me so uncomfortable and invalid. I can't even walk without feeling pain. And to run again? Maybe in a couple of months? God forbid ...

Before long, Travis arrived and it seemed that peace in the house reigned. I was happy to hear his voice. My heart soothed. I even got excited about going down to the kitchen. I slowly went down the stairs. The kids were around the kitchen table, waiting for their dad to set the pizza and salad. They were hungry.

"Baby, what are you doing down here? I was going to bring you dinner!"

"Thanks, Travis. Can I have a hug?"

When Travis hugged me, it felt like my world stopped right there. I cried. I don't know why. Maybe I know; One reason is because I don't seem to be helping anything and secondly, I'm thinking more than I should. I can't stop thinking about my neighbor Luke. I'm feeling guilty. My husband is an excellent companion and I am here with crazy thoughts about a young man.

"Baby. How are you? What's up?"

"Travis, I'm just tired of lying around doing nothing ..."

"Lori, you had an accident and it will pass. You don't have to be so sad like that."

"I'm sorry! I'm just a little down. Not running makes me sad."

"I know baby! Patience ..."

"Yes, Travis, you're right: patience!"

"Lori, sit with the kids and let's go to dinner.

Pizza and salad?

"Sure. Thank you, Travis!"

"You're welcome, my love."

Staying there with the kids was great. They talked about school, new friends, and sports. Travis told about his workday and new projects. Great to see everyone excited.

My mom called to check on me and talk a little bit about Thanksgiving.

"Mom, I think I'll be fine until October. Don't worry."

"If you want, I can go to Connecticut sooner and help you with the kids and the house."

"You don't have to, mom. Thank you. I know Dad doesn't like to be alone."

"But he will understand the situation."

"No mom, if I need it, I promise I'll let you know."

17 CHAPTER

After a week, I had an excellent improvement. I rested a lot and I can already walk better. My foot is still swollen, but it doesn't hurt as much as before. I can even already make dinner. When I went to the doctor, he said that I was recovering well and I could possibly start running soon. OMG! I cannot believe it! But let's go!

After the kids went to school and Travis went to work, I made coffee and sat in front of the house.

What a beautiful day! The sun was beautiful and not too hot. The sky was blue and the grass was freshly green. Incredible as it sounds, I felt a slight cold breeze on my face. The breeze was already bringing the chill of autumn. Looking at the leaves of the trees, it was already possible to see some slightly yellow leaves ... I closed my eyes and took a deep breath, thankful for my recovery.

It is so good to have health. Feeling the sunshine on my face brought me joy.

My warm coffee also brought peace. Everything is back to normal.

Suddenly, I see Luke approaching. This boy is handsome and it bothers me to be around him. I feel a great physical attraction for him.

"Good morning, Lori. Shall we run?"

"Good morning, Luke! I would like to, but I still can't."

"I know, I'm just playing with you."

"Do you need anything?"

"No! Thank you very much, Luke. Good run!"

"Thank you, Lori. I will."

And he went running. Even if I could run, I wouldn't run with him. This boy is a temptation.

I better get in and do the laundry.

Weeks went by and things were getting back to normal. I can already walk without limping. The pain in my foot didn't bother me much, but unfortunately, I still can't run.

Travis is super busy on his projects and the kids were already more involved with school activities and new friends.

With everything returning to normal, I started feeling lonely. A few times this week I called Travis, who was unable to attend. At night, at dinner, we talked, but Travis helped me quickly with the dishes and was ready to go back to the computer.

I think when I ran, it distracted me more. I was more involved with nature. I was happy.

"Baby, are you, all right?" Asked Travis.

"Yes, Travis, I'm fine. They're just a little distraught."

"Love, will you be able to finish the dishes? I need to finish a project and send it to Professor Russell today."

"Sure Travis. You can finish it. I'll finish the dishes."

"Lori, speaking of Professor Russell, he invited us to dinner at his house, as soon as you improve your foot."

"Wow, good! We will be happy to go."

Travis went back to his office.

As I finished the dishes, I remembered what happened to me today. Just remembering it made me lack air.

It was just a walk, but the guilt I'm feeling now is bothering me. I don't want to tell Travis, but not telling this to him seems like I'm hiding something from him.

18 CHAPTER

Motorcycle ride.

My morning started out normal: breakfast for the kids and Travis, laundry, and house cleaning. When I finished, I made tea and sat outside to enjoy the sun and the trees. Connecticut is so beautiful!

Trees upon more trees, especially in Woodbridge. Beautiful city.

When I sat down, I saw that Luke was returning from his morning run.

I was jealous.

Fifteen minutes passed and I continued to drink my tea, which was already cold. Feeling the light breeze in my hair and enjoying the sun.

Laura's garage opened and I saw that Luke was there starting his bike.

Luke was charming: sunglasses and dressed up to ride a motorcycle.

I saw from a distance that he saw me and waved at me. I tried not to look at him, but it was too late. I waved back.

To my surprise, he stopped at my garage and came walking. I was a little uncomfortable with the presence of him who soon came saying:

"Good morning Lori! How was your morning?"

"Good morning Luke! It was ok." I didn't want to lengthen the conversation.

"I imagine how difficult it must be for you to be at home all the time."

"Yes, Luke isn't easy. But I'll be fine soon to get back on track."

"For sure! Don't you want to take a motorcycle ride?"

"Oh no! I don't think so."

"The day is beautiful and it could distract you!"

"I do not know..."

"I have to take my resume to a company in New Haven and then we could go for a little break on East Haven beach."

"I don't think it's a good idea."

"I think you would love it. You don't have anything to do now, do you?"

"No, I don't. But I find it strange to ride a motorcycle with you."

"Strange, why? We are neighbors and you have not been out of the house for a long time. I promise you will be home in two hours."

And as incredible as it sounds, I went with Luke to ride a motorcycle. He went back to his house to get another helmet. He gave me the helmet and we left.

When we left, it was too late for me to go home. At the same time that I was there, within my own guilty thoughts, I was feeling like a teenager.

Luke's scent seems to have bewitched me. Hugging his body made me shiver. My God, what am I doing? Or what am I letting go?

I was shaking, I don't know if it was because of being there, or afraid of what might happen.

When Luke stopped by the company, I was waiting for him in the parking lot.

Out of fear or guilt, I called Travis. I spoke to the college receptionist and she told me that Travis was in a meeting. But she said she would send him a message to call me back.

By that time Luke was already returning.

"Ready! Shall we go to the beach?"

That was the answer that could have changed my life. If I had said "no better we back home", everything would have been different.

But even though I knew the risks, I said, "ok, let's go to the beach."

And it was from there that everything changed.

It was at that very moment that I knew my intentions: I wanted something more there. I wanted something much more dangerous, but I wasn't mature enough to make the right decision, both for my life and for Luke.

My big mistake.

When we were riding to the beach, I looked in the rearview of the motorcycle and saw how beautiful that boy was. He didn't look like a boy, but an extremely attractive man.

19 CHAPTER

Luke parked the bike and we went for a walk on the beach. I took off my shoes to feel the sand. The beach was beautiful.

The waves went and came very calmly. The sea breeze brought calmness and peace. The sun hitting my face seemed to bring strength to me. It felt like I was alive.

After walking for a while, my feet started to hurt.

"Hold my arm, Lori!" and so I did, I held Luke's arm. Strong arms that supported me during our walk.

Luke was telling me about his journey to look for work after he left college. How frustrated he was to still be living with his parents.

I loved listening to him ... while he spoke, I remembered myself when I left college, with all that anxiety to chase my dreams. Now, listening to Luke was funny, but I was enjoying that kind of conversation.

In my current life, I only talk about children, home, and family parties.

"Lori, are we going to sit on that rock over there?"

"Yes, Luke, let's go."

We settled on the stone and stood looking at that beautiful view of nature.

"Lori, I need to confess something to you ..."

At that moment I knew he was going to talk about us. The tone of his voice changed.

"You are a beautiful woman! I'm sorry, but I just wanted to make that comment."

"Okay Luke, thank you!"

"I hope these changes nothing between our friendship, okay?"

"Of course, not Luke ..."

I was silent and so was he.

Luke took my hand and kissed it. At that moment my legs shook. I knew and wanted a kiss to happen there. I was very attracted to him. I looked into the eyes of Luke who was already looking at me.

And it was at that moment that I felt his hands caressing my face. I closed my eyes and went towards Luke's lips. He gently touched my knees and it made me all but excited.

That's when my phone rang: it was Travis!

When I saw Travis' name there, on my cell phone, it looked like a bucket of cold water fell on my head. And it was at that moment that I saw what I was really doing.

My God! How selfish I was being. I was wanting to take advantage of a moment that could bring me so much suffering. Not just for me, but for my whole family.

"Luke, we need to go now!"

"Of course, Lori!"

At that moment, it seems that Luke was scared too. He was involved there, wanting something that was impossible: a relationship with a married woman.

We went home quietly.

When we stopped at home, I got off the bike and gave him my helmet. We looked at each other as if we were having an unresolved case. He wanted to say something, but he said nothing. I went home.

20 CHAPTER

I went into the house. My breath was fast. I crouched at the door, put my hand on my head, and remembered what had happened. Or what could have happened?

Travis called me again because I didn't answer him when he called me at the beach.

If I talk to Travis now, I don't know what to say to him. Do I tell him I went to the beach with our young neighbor? No, I can't!

I got up and went to the kitchen. I took a glass and filled it with lemonade and drank it. It seems to have refreshed me, but it didn't refresh my guilt.

After cooling my head, I called Travis back. I had even forgotten what I needed to talk to him about.

Travis was busy when I returned the call. So we didn't talk that afternoon.

I started making a snack for the kids when they got back from school.

My head wouldn't stop ... My God! Because I went on that bike, Luke certainly realized that I was interested in him.

Around three o'clock in the afternoon, my children arrived from school.

As usual, they ate and each of them went to their room.

And I stayed there with my guilt, preparing dinner.

When Travis came home from work, he kissed me and went to his office. I set the table and around six-thirty in the afternoon, I called the kids and Travis to dinner.

I ended my night doing the dishes alone, again, and Travis in the office ...

As soon as I finished the dishes and folded the clothes that were in the laundry, I went to take a shower.

When I took my clothes off, I looked at myself in the mirror and wondered if Luke would be excited to see me naked.

I tried all afternoon to get that boy out of my head, but it looks like I'm looking forward to seeing him now ... my God! Help me get these sinful thoughts out of my head ... please!

While I was there thinking about Luke, Travis arrived in our room.

"Baby, do you think that next week I can arrange our dinner with Professor Russell?"

"Yes, Travis, of course. My foot is already getting much better. Maybe I won't be able to wear high heels, but that's it."

"Wow, Lori! Are you naked waiting for me?"

I smiled, but that was not my intention. Travis came up behind me and said:

"I'm a lucky man! I have the hottest woman in the world."

Travis's hand started to caress me and that turned me on ... we started kissing and I started taking off his pants. I put my hand on his body and had oral sex with him. He went crazy ... and we went to bed to make delicious love. I needed sex today ... It calmed my soul.

Travis and I stayed there in bed, resting a little bit from sex. I looked at him and realized that I still loved him. And that I want him still close to me. I love having sex with him. But why am I like this with Luke?

I can't throw my life all away because of my stupid adventure.

We kissed and went to shower together. Travis is an excellent friend, husband, and companion. But I think lately he's been working hard and leaving me alone. I am feeling very alone. If I tell Travis that, he might feel guilty and try to prolong his projects to stay with me longer.

I can't disrupt his career. Mainly, now that everything seems to be going very well in college, I cannot come up with this problem.

That night we slept and cuddled. That was great!

21 CHAPTER

Days passed and life went on. In those days, I talked more with my mom to put the Thanksgiving prep plans in order.

Every day after the kids and Travis left, I made coffee and stood at the window looking out. I saw that Luke was running, looked at my house, almost stopped, but continued running.

But, one morning, someone knocked on the door. My heart shook because I thought it was Luke, but it was just the postwoman who came to deliver me some boxes.

"Good morning, Mrs. Anderson! Some boxes for you."

"Good morning! Thank you so much. I was expecting these boxes. It will be for Thanksgiving ..."

"Beautiful day out here today, isn't it?"

She commented while I signed the receipt for the boxes.

When I looked up to deliver the woman from the post office, I saw that Luke was already approaching the door.

"Good morning ladies!"

"Good Morning." Replied the woman at the post office. I was silent.

"Lori, do you want help with the boxes?"

"I don't think it will be necessary, thank you."

"What is it, Lori? I can help you ..."

No Luke, you can only help by getting away from me ... This is the only help I need from you. I thought…

And so, it was, Luke helped me with the boxes. He was simply super sexy: very athletic. I didn't even look at him much.

"Lori, I have something new!"

"Really, Luke, what is it?

"I was hired by the company that we went to take my resume for that day at the beach."

"Wow, how cool, congratulations!"

"You brought me luck, Lori."

"Do you accept water, Luke?"

"Yes, please, it's hot outside today. I ran about six miles this morning."

I asked Luke to leave the boxes on the kitchen table and went to get him a glass of water. When I delivered the glass of water, we looked into each other's eyes.

"Lori, I'm sorry about that day. I lost control. You are a very attractive woman."

"Okay, Luke."

Even though he said that he touched my hand and kissed it.

I was a little stunned and confused, and in that mixture of feelings, he kissed me. The worst part was that he didn't even force it.

I kissed him back. That kiss was reciprocal.

Our lips slowly touched at first, but after a few seconds, it felt like everything was on fire. My body didn't even seem to be my own body ... I was out of control. It felt like that was my last kiss. Hot and fiery kiss.

That is good.

Luke hugged me, placing my body next to his, and I could smell those muscles, that smell. Giddily, he sat me on the kitchen island and stood between my legs. I could feel his penis hard. Then, I could feel his hand going up inside my shirt and touching my nipples.

When he touched my nipples, I felt a heat rising inside me.

I put my hand on his hard penis.

He laid me down on the kitchen island and took off my panties and gave me oral sex. When that happened, I had some orgasms and I knew I was going to make love to him. I had no strength. My body was given over to him.

Luke and I looked like two in love, but that sex was everything. I can't describe that feeling. I could see stars while he was licking me.

Then he dropped me off the kitchen island, turned me offshore and penetrated me. I felt so many orgasms at that time that I got tired …

When we finished, our great sexual adventure, we embraced. I was tired.

After carnal pleasure, reason came. Reason for integrity and being faithful also came. I realized my big mistake, but it was too late.

"Luke, please go away."

"How are you, Lori?"

"Luke, are you crazy? I'm a married woman and did you see what we just did?"

"Easy, Lori, easy! Everything will be fine …"

"Luke, get out of my house, now, please!"

He was stunned, took his shirt and slammed the door.

My God! This could not have happened … not really.

I decided to take a shower to cool my head

and maybe wash off my body.

The guilt of that betrayal? Yes, and a lot of guilt, but the feeling of seeing Luke's face, was the best sight I could remember.

22 CHAPTER

Travis came home early today because we are going to dinner at Mr. Russel's house.

I went to the salon in the afternoon to get my nails and hair done.

When Travis opened the door, I felt so guilty about what had happened between me and Luke, that I lowered my head.

"Hi love, how are you?"

"Hi Travis, I am fine."

"I love your hair; it looks really good."

"Thank you, Travis. Your suit is ready in the bedroom. I chose a tie for you, but there are others in your closet if you want to change."

"Lori, my love, you always choose the best ties for me ... thanks, baby."

"Okay!"

While Travis showered, I put on makeup and then put on my dress.

"Travis, I'm waiting for you down there, okay?"

"Sure! I'll be ready quickly."

I ordered pizza for Cody and Valerie and told them to call me if anything was needed.

Travis came down, we said goodbye to the kids, and off we went.

When we were leaving, I saw that Luke was on the motorcycle arriving at his house. I lacked breath. What a horrible feeling that was.

Travis stopped the car to greet him:

"Hello, Luke, how are you? How are your parents?"

I didn't even look out of our car window. I just stood there and looked ahead.

"Hi Travis, I'm fine, thanks. My parents are fine, too."

"Greet them for me. Have a great night, Luke."

"The same for you, a great night."

And Travis drove out.

"This boy looks like a good boy, don't you think, baby?"

"Yes, Travis, it seems to be."

"Are you all right, Lori?"

"Yes, honey, I just had a headache this afternoon, but that's it."

"Russell is super excited about this dinner."

"Will it be all four of us or will there be other guests?"

"I believe there will be other guests."

"Travis, do you think this high heel is okay?"

"Everything about you is perfect, baby."

"You are also super stylish, Travis."

"Thank you, my love."

And we go to dinner.

During the trip, until we arrived at dinner, I listened to Travis and all his excitement about the new projects that he proposed.

When we arrived at Russell's house, we were so well received. Russell's wife, Heather, was super nice. The table and appetizers were well organized. There was even a waitress, who soon brought us wine. Travis and I were introduced to other guests who also worked at the college. All pleasant and receptive.

23 CHAPTER

"So, Lori, how are you feeling living in Connecticut?" Heather asked me, while Russell went out with Travis to talk to the other guests.

I think this dinner will help distract me a little. Seeing new people will help me feel better. Or at least, forget what happened.

"Heather, I'm just loving it. Aside from my accident with my foot, everything is going very well."

"True, Russell commented about your accident. I'm sorry."

"Thank you, but I'm much better now."

"That's great! And your kids, are you enjoying school?"

"Yes, a lot. They adapted very well."

"That sounds great Lori! I'm super happy for you."

"Thank you, Heather."

"Excuse me, Lori, I'll have a look at dinner and I'll be right back."

"Yes, of course, feel free. I'll be fine."

Soon another lady came and we started talking. The night was definitely a delight. Incredible and nice people that made me breathe a little.

It was also nice to see how happy and fulfilled Travis was.

I've never seen Travis so communicative. He smiled all the time, and I even though he drank even more than he should have, but it was okay. It was his night.

Before dinner time, Russell again introduced Travis and me and praised the work Travis is doing in college and how much it would bring prestige and empowerment to college.

At that moment, all the sacrifice of changing the state and being away from our family members was worth it: Travis' dream was coming true.

Everyone present at dinner applauded Travis for his performance. At that moment, Travis stood up and spoke to everyone:

"This moment is incredibly special for me and my family. All these years of dedication to my professional career and today I can say that it is succeeding, it would not be possible if it were not for my wife Lori."

Everyone applauded him. The wives murmured "aww, that's lovely!"

Travis kept talking and looked into my eyes:

"Thank you, Lori, for your love and dedication to our family. Without you, I couldn't be here! I love you!"

I was incredibly happy with Travis' testimony and his recognition of my dedication to all these years.

I got up and gave a simple kiss on Travis.

I was a little embarrassed, but happy at that moment. Travis was very elegant with the sweet words about my collaboration in his professional life. I was grateful.

After all the speeches, we all sat down and dinner was served.

The salad was wonderful. Soon after, the main dish "Baked Dijon Salmon" was served, just perfect.

"Are you happy, Lori?"

"Of course, Travis! Congratulations on your success and thanks for the words."

"You can't imagine how important you are in my career. Without you, I couldn't get here."

"Travis, you are an excellent professional. You would make it to the top with me or alone."

"It may even be Lori. But I always dreamed of having a family. And you practically take care of the children alone."

"You help me a lot, Travis."

"I can even help, my love, but you are in front of the house and I am grateful for that."

"We are a team, Travis!"

"Yes, baby, we are. And how are the preparations for Thanksgiving?"

"It's all under control, so far. I just want to

organize where our parents are going to sleep."

"In the basement?"

"I think it would be a great idea because there is a bathroom there and that can give them some comfort."

"But we only have one room ..."

"Yes, Travis. Maybe do some division in that lighter area of the basement. Put a bed there and leave everything set up for future occasions."

"Great idea, Lori!"

Travis and I talked a little more and then dessert came. Everything at dinner at Mr. Russell and Heather's was incredibly well organized.

I was paying close attention because I already know that soon, I will have to organize a dinner for them. I already know that Travis is going to make a point of inviting them to dinner at our house.

We finished dessert and went back to the living room for a few last words. Coming to this dinner today was particularly good for me: it made me remember who I am. I am married to an excellent man, an excellent professional, and the father of my children whom I love very much. My life has a focus, and I can't let an attraction to a young boy take me out of my future.

This afternoon's sin still burns in my body. I can't forget for a second about Luke, how we made love ... My God don't let this get in the way of my life.

But for a second, I remembered Luke squeezing and pulling me towards him. I smiled and breathed ...

"Okay baby, why are you laughing?"

"Hi Travis, nothing! Just reminded me of something funny. Shall we go?"

"Yes, let's just say goodbye to them, and let's go."

So it was. We said goodbye to Russel and Heather and took the road home.

Today was a great night. Travis was overjoyed ... It was good to see him like this.

24 CHAPTER

When we were almost home, Travis commented that he might have to make a trip to Europe. He explained that it could happen before or right after thanksgiving and he would be back a week before Christmas.

"Wow, Travis! You never stayed out that long. Almost a month!"

"I know baby! But the project must have support from a college in England."

"Wow! What can I do?"

"I need their support both financially and scientifically. And the College of England was extremely interested."

"Okay, Travis. I was looking to apply for an art teaching position at the local high school."

"Wait for next year, Lori. This year has brought a lot of changes. The kids and I really need your support."

"I think it would be better to apply next year."

"Do you need money or something, baby?"

"No, Travis, I don't need anything. I just wanted to feel more productive. Sometimes I feel a little useless."

"What is it, my angel! Are you useless? No one is as busy as you are!"

"Okay, Travis. Just know that I will need to find some work soon, okay?"

"Sure, sure! Everything will happen at the right time, Lori."

After this conversation with Travis, I was really upset. I wasn't upset with Travis, but I was upset with me. Whenever I want to work, Travis always finds an excuse, and I accept his excuses.

We got home and went to check on the kids in their rooms. I went to take off my makeup and take a shower.

I heard that Travis brushed his teeth and went to bed. I don't know why, but there was agony in thinking about the possibility that Travis is with a lover.

He always arrives later, and now he is leaving for this trip for almost a month? I don't know, it's very strange that I feel this sensation.

After what happened to me and Luke today, anything is possible in the life of a married couple.

But I can't even imagine that Travis is having an affair. No, no ... I think I'm feeling guilty about all that happened between me and Luke. I'm trying to find things that don't exist.

When I got out of the shower and went to bed, Travis was already asleep.

I woke up early to make breakfast for Cody and Valerie. Later, I realized that Travis didn't get up when he always does and I went to call him:

"Travis, Travis it's time to get up."

"Good morning, my beauty! Did you sleep well?"

"Yes, I slept. The breakfast is ready."

Lori, today I'm staying at home with you! I took the day off."

"What miracle is that?"

"Are we going to have coffee together at the Omni Hotel today?"

"Yes, let's go ... it took me by surprise but then I organized the kitchen and did the laundry."

Okay, I'll wait for you."

"I'm just going to say goodbye to the children and I will get ready quickly, okay?

"Sure!"

25 CHAPTER

After the kids left on the bus to school, I quickly cleaned up the kitchen and went to the bedroom to get ready.

"Travis, I'm surprised you are taking a day off!"

"I've been working a lot Lori and I want to spend the day with you. Let's have breakfast together and go for a walk on the beach."

"Very good!"

And we got ready and went to breakfast.

We left to the hotel for our breakfast.

Travis commented on how much he enjoyed the dinner and how nice the people at the party were.

As we rounded the corner, I saw Luke returning from his morning run. In fact, he was a little earlier than usual. Maybe, he starts working today. My God, what does that matter to me! I'm going to have breakfast with my husband and I'm here imagining things.

I turned my attention back to Travis and started giving my opinion about the dinner yesterday. Really, everything was perfect. Russell and Heather were great hosts!

"Lori, do you know that I love you very much?"

"Yes, Travis, I think."

"Being with you in my spare time is all I want."

"Next year, we could go to Europe, just the two of us. What do you think about that, Travis?"

"Excellent idea, Lori!"

And so, we went to our breakfast, exchanging ideas and planning for our future.

As soon as we sat at the hotel table to have our breakfast, they brought us coffee. I took advantage of the fact that Travis was relaxed to bring up the subject of me going back to work. I definitely need to occupy my time. I can't stay at home doing anything! Especially with Luke around.

"My love, we already talked about it!"

"Please, Travis, at least think about it."

"Lori, we've talked about this so many times. For our family today, it's important to have you as support. You had agreed with that idea."

"Yes, I did, but the kids are already older, and maybe if I worked at least part time ..."

"Lori, when I get back from my trip to Europe, we can talk then. But, now let's enjoy our morning."

"Okay, Travis. Let's enjoy our breakfast, which looks wonderful."

I already know that Travis will find all the excuses for me to not go to work.

My morning with Travis was great. It has been a while since we have been out to talk.

After breakfast, we went for a walk on the beach. The sun was strong, but the breeze was cool. We took off our shoes and walked with our feet in the sand. It is refreshing to be around nature.

Before going home, I stopped by the

supermarket to buy some fruits and vegetables for the house. As soon as we parked at home, I put away the groceries while Travis stayed in the garage fixing a mess that had been around since our move.

I heard someone talking to him outside and it was Laura, our neighbor. I heard that Travis agreed to something with Laura, but I didn't hear what it was.

"Baby, Laura called us this afternoon for a cookout. I agreed, okay?"

"Travis, I don't know if it's a good idea."

"She said that her son started working in a great position and they wanted to celebrate with our family here."

"I would rather not go ..."

"Should I go there and say that you had made other plans?"

"That would be a little rude to her, don't you think?"

"I think it is rude, mainly, because she gave you the most support when you had a swollen foot."

"At least we had a lot of banana bread, right?"

"Lori, it will be good, at least you won't even need to prepare the dinner ..."

I ended up agreeing not to look boring.

I prepared a snack for the children when they arrived and I went to do laundry.

Travis was still in the garage fixing things up, much to my amazement. He never stays long in any place, if not in his office to study.

My heart was tight in knowing that I was going to see Luke. The guilt will not leave me alone.

I'm very embarrassed to go with Travis in this situation. I hope everything goes well, and that Luke forgets everything that happened yesterday between us.

That is the only thing I can wish for.

I'm bringing grapes and strawberries for Laura's cookout.

What a terrible situation I created!!!

So, the kids came home from school. Travis finished what he was doing in the garage and my mom was texting me to finish the Thanksgiving menu.

What a noisy house of mine! Maybe all of this gets Luke out of my head.

26 CHAPTER

At about five in the afternoon, we went to the cookout to celebrate Luke's new job.

Everyone was there, except Luke. That afternoon, I met Laura and Chris' parents who were also there to celebrate their grandson's success.

All of them were genuinely nice. Chris was at the grill preparing hot dogs and hamburgers.

Laura made a fruit table while my grapes and strawberries also helped to color the table. Laura decorated her back yard with a message to Luke wishing him luck in his new career. I think Luke graduated in business administration and this job coincides with his dream and his professional career.

"Lori, thank you so much for the fruits! They are super fresh !!!"

"I'm glad you liked Laura!"

"Thanks for coming, Luke will be surprised!"

"Doesn't he know about the party here?"

"He doesn't know! Surprise! He started at work today, and Chris loves to celebrate!"

"Yes, it's very important to celebrate big events."

"Please, Lori, feel free! I'll get the bread for Chris and I'll be right back!"

"Do you need any help?"

"No, Lori thanks... I'll be back ..."

Travis stayed around talking to Chris about his trip to Europe and I went to talk to Laura's mom. The kids were in the basement playing video games when I heard the noise of the bike coming. I had the impression that my face was red, but I kept talking to Laura's mother.

I noticed that Luke said something to his mother and smiled loudly. When he was approaching the backyard, everyone went to congratulate him on the new job. I went too. Getting closer to him, I saw that he was with a woman. I had never seen this person around or at Laura's house before.

It was a beautiful girl. She was in her early twenties. When I looked at Luke, I saw that he was a little uncomfortable seeing me. He hugged me and thanked me for the visit, then immediately went to hug his grandfather. The girl was holding hands with Luke and he never let go of her hand.

I couldn't believe my reaction: it felt like I was jealous!

My God! What's happening to me?

After everyone greeted Luke, he went to take a shower and the girl went with him. I continued my conversation with Laura's mother.

I don't remember my conversation from that afternoon ... I was in shock.

First, because I saw Luke and I felt an emotion ... Second, Luke arrived with this girl. Is this girl his girlfriend?

If so, he has no shame on his face!!! He came to my place and ... but he didn't make me make love to him. I wanted to.

When Luke looked at me it was super cold and it looked like he was sorry for what happened between us.

I felt like crap at that moment.

In all this mixture of feelings of guilt, shame, and fear, Travis arrived with a plate of hamburger and fruits for me.

"Lori, eat something. You only had breakfast today."

"True, Travis, I think that's why I'm not feeling very well."

"Shall we sit at that table?"

"Yes, have you eaten Travis?"

"Not yet I'll be right back. I'll call the kids first."

And Travis went to the basement to ask the kids to eat when Luke sat at my table.

"Lori, don't think about me with this girl. She is a friend."

"Luke, please get away from my table."

"Calm down Lori. Nobody knows anything. I just want you to know that I really want you."

And Luke got up smiling and went to talk to

the people at the party. Travis then sat with me to eat and talk.

I was relieved by Luke's words. He could be lying to me, but just his affection for caring about me, made me calm down.

Luke is driving me crazy. When would I ever feel like this in life?

I'm loving it all and I need to be mature to not let things go out of place.

Imagine if Travis even thought about it? My children? My family?

Travis and I finished our hamburger and went to stay close to the kids. Everywhere I went, I saw that Luke followed me with his eyes. This flirting got me excited. What a temptation, this boy.

Where is my dignity, fidelity, or morality at that moment, my God!

Luke lied to me about the girl. She stayed with him all the time. They talked and smiled at each other. But I felt special for Luke. I know he loses control when I'm around. I realized it today.

After an hour, we went home. The kids have school tomorrow.

"Thank you so much, Laura! The party for Luke was great and the cookout was delicious."

"Thank you! It's great to have you as neighbors. Kind people."

"Good evening everyone."

"Good evening." Everyone who was at Laura's party gently answered us.

Cody and Valerie were sleepy. They could have gone home alone, but I didn't want to be at the party looking at Luke with his girlfriend.

27 CHAPTER

The days went by and Thanksgiving was already coming. My family and Travis's family were due to arrive home a week before Thanksgiving.

I was on the run with the housework. Cody decided to play soccer and that made me busier with schedules. The weekend always had soccer and I was the one who took him to the tournaments.

I organized the basement for my parents. It was excellent. Travis' parents will sleep in the guest room.

Travis was so anxious about his trip to Europe. Travis's trip was scheduled for the first of December and returned on the twenty-third of December.

Maybe my parents will be here at home for Christmas since Travis will be out of the country and they want to be with the kids. My dad said he wants to help with Cody's soccer.

Luke and I are still seeing each other. After his party to celebrate his new job, we met a couple of times. Both he and I are terribly busy.

As for us, me and Luke, it's a mixture of guilt and passion. Being with Luke makes me feel alive. I feel like a woman. When I'm with Travis, it seems like the only thing I serve is to help everyone in the house. My personal and professional life does not seem to exist. I feel so guilty about this double life ... but Luke makes me feel happy ...

In one of my meetings with Luke, it was exceptionally good. We met in a small hotel near his work. Luke brought me roses. He is very affectionate.

We kissed, and since we didn't have much time, we made love without many conversations.

"Lori, I love being with you."

"Also, I like being with you, Luke."

And we kissed ...

Our meetings were usually about kissing and

bodies. Sex was our priority.

After some meetings between me and Luke, I decided to enjoy the moment. I don't have time to decide or think about my actions. I just want Travis to never find that out.

I hope that someday Luke will be able to go somewhere else and leave me alone. My biggest anguish is because I also want to meet Luke, I want to kiss him, and make love to him. I don't want to lose Luke.

Sometimes, I find myself dreaming of going out with Luke and having wine with him and talking to him all night.

I don't know what to do for now, but my soul is tied to Luke.

About my husband, I still love him. I can't explain it, but I still love Travis.

"Lori? Baby?"

"Yes, Travis!"

"I was hoping you could possibly pack my bags. I still need to finish some of my thesis before I leave."

"Of course, I can. How many suits will you

need?"

"Love, I think about four. Pajamas, socks, and underwear."

"Leave it, I'll pack your bags." It looks like Travis once packed his bags. I laughed to myself.

I'm packing Travis' bags ten days before the trip, but I'm going to do this so he can enjoy Thanksgiving and not be stressed.

"Lori, what time will our parents arrive tomorrow?"

Shouted Travis from his office.

"Two o'clock in the afternoon. At Bradley Airport, Hartford ..."

"Will you be able to pick them up, my love. I'll be busy at that time."

"I will go."

"I am sorry, Lori. But I need to finish everything before the trip ... I promise when I get back from England, we will take a week off. Just you and me."

I didn't even answer Travis ... I think I got annoyed because Travis won't be able to pick up our parents at the airport. I will need to wake up early and have lunch ready so that when we get from the airport they can eat.

As I folded Travis's clothes, I heard Luke's motorcycle passing down the street. I went up to the window to see if I could see him a little bit. But I think Luke drove fast because when I got to the window, he was already gone. I felt my heart flutter ...

I became a wife again ...

I finished organizing Travis's things for his trip and went to prepare dinner when someone knocked on the door. When I opened the door, I almost had an attack. It was from Luke. With that beautiful smile on his face.

"Hi Lori, how are you?"

"Hi Luke, I'm fine"

"My mom asked me to bring this banana cake."

"Wow, how nice ... it will be our dessert!"

At that moment, Luke came awfully close to my ear and said lovingly "I miss you, Lori."

I quickly pushed him away from me. I smiled at him, but my face went red and my breath went fast. I was agonized thinking that Travis could see him whispering in my ear.

I went to the kitchen and Luke came after me. Afraid that Luke would try to hug me or try to kiss me, I called Travis.

"Travis, Luke is here! He came to bring a banana cake."

And I looked at Luke, disapproving him of any attitude towards me. I realized that Luke was disappointed that Travis was at home.

"Hi Luke, how are you?"

"Hi Travis, I'm fine."

"And the new job, are you enjoying it?"

"Yes, Travis, I think it is incredibly good. This work is fitting with the projects I have for my professional career in the future."

"Very good, Luke! Investing in your professional dream is very good and will bring excellent results."

They talked while I prepared dinner. I don't know what the moment was, but Travis commented to Luke that he would be traveling to Europe and would be gone for a few days. When Travis finished telling him about his trip, I looked at Luke, and Luke looked at me with a happy look ... like he meant "we'll be free."

At that moment I felt happy and at the same time, as always, guilt. How could I let that happen ...? I have a lover!!!

I tried to hide from myself that I have a lover. I tried to blame Travis for not letting me work, or because I am alone, but in truth, it is all my fault. And I want to continue with all of this! Until when my God?

After they talked, Luke left. Travis went back to the office.

I stay there in the kitchen, confused by my attitudes, confused by my feelings... Who am I becoming?

28 CHAPTER

I woke up earlier than usual today. I made breakfast and [started the laundry soon after.

The children woke up, had breakfast, and went to school. Travis showered and got dressed. He had coffee and went to work. Before Travis left, I asked him to come back earlier today to help me with dinner.

I cleaned the whole house so that when our parents arrived, everything would look perfect.

I made chicken roast for lunch. I left some vegetables ready to cook for when we arrived from the airport.

Around eleven o'clock, I left Woodbridge and drove to Hartford. At this time, the traffic was very congested. I will probably spend some time in traffic ... about two hours before I get to the airport. I went to a florist in North Haven and bought two flower bouquets: one for my mother and one for my mother-in-law.

I arrived at around one in the afternoon, earlier than I imagined.

I stayed around the airport and remembered when Travis, the kids, and I arrived here in Connecticut. At that time, we were so anxious. Moving to Connecticut was an excellent project, I think.

I looked on the screen and saw that the plane had landed. I felt happiness at that moment.

Some time passed and soon, I saw my mother waving her hand with a huge smile. Good to see our people!!! Then I saw my father and Travis' parents.

They were all smiling. I should have brought Cody and Valerie. Surely, they would be even happier. They must miss them more than they miss me and Travis.

"Hi, people! How wonderful to have you here in Connecticut!"

"My daughter, I miss you! You look beautiful!"

"Thank you, mom, hi daddy! How long has

it been?"

"Hi, my daughter. It's been a really long time ...."

I handed the flowers to my mother and mother-in-law. They were super happy.

And so were our exchanges of longing. My in-laws were as loving as ever. It was a great reception.

We took their luggage and went home. Good thing that the traffic wasn't too bad. It took us about an hour to get home.

When arriving home, they started to comment: "wow what a beautiful place !!!"

Yes, Connecticut is an incredibly beautiful state, especially Woodbridge.

When we got home, they were delighted with our decorations and were happy to know that we were doing well. As soon as I parked the car, I saw that Luke had also arrived at his house. Strange, Luke arrived earlier today.

So, I stopped the car and we entered the house. I told them that we could get our suitcases after.

I put the chicken to heat and put the vegetables in the kitchen. I also made mashed potatoes.

We stayed there in the kitchen. I served them red wine while I finished lunch. I set the table and we stayed there in the kitchen talking.

Soon, Travis arrived.

"Wow, my daughter! I miss my grandchildren so much! What time do they arrive?" My mother asked.

"Mom, in about forty minutes."

"How was the trip to Connecticut?" Travis asked as I took the chicken out of the oven. My mom came to help me with the vegetables.

"It was excellent, my son." Replied Travis's father.

While I was putting food on the table, Travis kept talking to them about his projects and telling him about his trip to Europe. How good it is to have a family at home. We feel love and comfort with the exchange of information in our lives. Especially in our case, we changed our lives to pursue other dreams.

Just when I finished putting lunch on the

table and our parents sat down, the kids arrived. It was another party! Travis had to go in the car to get their bags because the children's gifts were there. Then I called everyone to have lunch before the lunch got cold. The children wanted to open the presents and I asked them to have lunch first. They could sit in the living room to open the presents after. Then, everyone agreed.

29 CHAPTER

We all sat in the dining room. A big family with lots of love.

I looked at every face there. My parents, children, Travis, and Travis's parents; but my gaze left the window of my house and went to Luke's house. What would happened with my family if they find out about Luke?

Am I thinking of some crazy change in my life?

While I was thinking about Luke, at that incredibly special moment, my mother called me twice ... and I was wandering in my baseless dreams.

"Lori? Your mom is asking you!" Said Travis.

I was startled by my lack of attention and apologized.

"Sorry, mom, what is it?"

"What is on your mind?"

"I remembered that I forgot to buy more fruit ..."

"I can go shopping," Travis added.

"Don't worry, I can buy another day. But mom, what did you ask."

"Yes, daughter, it was about Thanksgiving ... Is everything in order, or do we need anything else?"

"This is all ready, Mom! Thank you."

"We want to help on Thanksgiving ... I can cook the turkey!" Said Travis' mother.

"Great then, Susan ... you will cook the turkey, which is the most delicious of all."

"Hey, this makes me jealous." My mother said with a smile. I think the wine made everyone happy.

As we sat around the table talking, Luke texted me:

"Hi Lori. I rented an apartment in downtown New Haven. Could you come with me to help decorate?"

"Hi Luke, I'm sorry I have a full house. My parents arrived from Colorado for Thanksgiving."

"How cool! It could be another day."

"Okay Luke, maybe tomorrow, ok?"

"Sure, enjoy your family."

Luke upsets me so much. Maybe it is because I wanted to go with him now to see his new apartment. Or maybe because he didn't move to this apartment before we moved here.

Now I have this problem. I think I'm in love with him. My life has not been exciting for a long time and this boy appeared to turn my life upside down.

We finished our lunch and my parents and in-laws went to bed for a while.

They were exhausted from the trip and also from the wine ...

"Baby, I'm going to help you in the kitchen."

"Thanks, Travis."

"How are you, honey?"

"I am good."

"You are so quiet."

"I think I'm tired."

After we finished washing the dishes and organizing everything, we went to bed. I was exhausted.

Early in the morning, everyone was awake. My mom decided to take a walk around the neighbors with my dad. Travis' mother and I went to prepare breakfast for everyone. The kids were still waking up and getting ready to go to school.

"Lori, your home is so beautiful and comfortable. Everything is so beautiful and organized!"

"Thanks, Susan! I try to make the house very cozy."

"What about your foot, Lori? Can you run again already?"

"Susan, I'm walking. But I feel a little bit of pain. I can't run like I used to."

"Wow, Lori! What a pity, isn't it? I wonder how hard this is for you."

"Susan, it really is. When I ran, I felt really good. I had to change my routine a little to accept this new Lori!"

"I hope your foot will be fine soon!"

"Thanks, Susan, I hope so too!"

Travis and his father were talking in the garden. I assume Travis was telling him about his success at the new job here.

We put the breakfast on the table and everyone sat down. We waited for my mom and dad to arrive from the walk.

I sent a message to Luke that I could stop by his apartment at about eleven-thirty and if that time would be possible. He immediately replied that he would be waiting for me.

I smiled slightly at myself, feeling joy in his response. My parents arrived and we had breakfast that looked more like a party. Travis went to work

128

and left the kids at school.

We cleaned up the breakfast mess and I told my mom that I would have to leave around ten-thirty. She just answered ok.

So, I spent the morning with my family; cleaning the house, and then sitting down to have tea and talk.

I took the opportunity to change and leave. I said goodbye to everyone and left:

"Lori, will you be able to go to the market to buy some chips and vegetables when you get back?"

"Sure mom! I won't be long; I'll be back by one o'clock in the afternoon."

And I left my home.

As I drove towards Luke's apartment, a million thoughts went through my head. I was wondering what I really wanted to do with my life. I wanted to be with Luke, but I wasn't thinking about the consequences of that. Going to be with Luke was a moment of mine and I really wanted it.

I made a fool of myself and I didn't even

care. I wanted to check it out and be with him. I felt like I was alive with him. I could even tell him about my dreams. If I tell Travis my dreams, he immediately cuts everything off saying that I need to be home for family support.

I understood about being there with the children when they were younger, but now that they are older, I don't see the need to stay home all the time.

I want and need to live!!!

Travis and I decided that I need to stay home, but I do not want to listen.

Perhaps moving here has affected my personal life. Maybe I'm unhappy or I haven't found myself as a person yet. I keep trying to find answers. Is Luke my answer? Or an excuse for my insecurities?

30 CHAPTER

I arrived at the building where Luke moved. I felt a shiver in my spine. I do not know if it is fear or if it is excitement! The only certainty I have now is that this visit today is a mistake, but an adventure.

I sent him a text saying that I was already at the address. I asked him if I would go up or we would go straight to the store to buy the decorations.

"Hi, Lori! Come up to see the space. Then we'll go."

"Okay, I'm going up then!"

And I went, took the elevator, and stopped

on his floor.

When the elevator door opened, he was already there with that beautiful smile on his face. We hugged and then kissed. I think it's so good to feel Luke's arms. A weightless embrace from years of relationship. It seems that I feel everything new: love, joy, and smiling again.

I'm happy with Luke.

We entered the apartment and it was very spacious and elegant. I went into the rooms and everything was clean and organized. There were two large windows in the living room and the kitchen was quite large. The space was open and gave the impression that the kitchen was large.

"So, did you like our apartment, Lori?"

I leaned against the kitchen island and was startled by Luke's question.

"How? Our apartment?"

"Yes, I rented it first because I want to start my life and have space for us."

"Luke, you know I'm a married woman, right?"

As I tried to talk to Luke, he was coming

very slowly, close to me. And I can't resist that person. Luke is very attractive and knows how to get to a woman. He's young, but he has a magic that I can't explain or resist.

And kissed me before answering me. What a kiss, my God! Hot kisses that make my legs shake, get wet and I lose my breath.

"Yes, I know that you are married, which is a great sadness!"

I smiled, but I was handed over to Luke's arms. And right there in the kitchen, we made love. How wonderful to feel his weight on me. Feeling his hands take off my clothes and his tongue travels over my body. He gives me oral sex as no one has ever done to me.

It warms me up, makes me happy, and makes me reach orgasm fast. This man drives me crazy.

At certain times, I thought I no longer felt so much pleasure in having sex with Travis.

Of course, everyday life in a couple's relationship is tiring, but I don't have as much sexual attraction for Travis as I used to.

My biggest mistake was staying with Luke like that. But our attraction was very great from the beginning and today I cannot resist this man.

Making love or having sex with Luke makes me very relaxed. It seems that the world is in my favor. My body looks good and my head only thinks about positive things.

"Lori, you are a sexy and beautiful woman. Your body, your smell makes me crazy. No man can resist you!"

I love it when Luke looks at me. He seems to want me so much that just seeing him want me, makes me excited. I feel beautiful. I feel sexy. I feel alive.

Those words from Luke to me, make me feel like the most desired woman on this planet. Maybe that is one of the things I want to hear and that makes me want Luke.

After a morning of love, Luke and I went to take a shower in his new bathroom. He asked to wash my hair and we had a lot of fun.

Then we went to Milford. I went in my car and him on the motorcycle as I needed to go straight home after.

We stopped at a furniture store.

"Luke, I don't have much time. Let's look at the living room today and maybe look at your bedroom decorations another time?"

"You mean, our bedroom, right?

Luke said as he hugged me. It was in public and I didn't even care.

We went into the furniture store and right away Luke liked the living room.

Everything was white and modern.

"Lori, I loved this room. I like everything clear, what do you think?"

"Luke, great taste. I think it will look perfect in the living room of your apartment."

"You see, Lori! We match everything!"

Delighted by Luke's happiness, I hugged him and we gave a light kiss on the lips.

When suddenly, I heard:

"Luke? Son?"

"Hi, mom! What are you doing here?"

"Well, I came here to buy some things for your apartment. Hello Lori!"

"Hi, Laura!"

My God, now what? What a super embarrassing situation ... Did Laura see us kissing?

"I'm surprised, Luke! I didn't know that you and Lori were so close?"

My face got red. I felt that all the blood in my body went to my face. What a situation!

"Yes, mom, we are friends. I even asked Lori to come with me here today, to help me decorate the apartment. Her house is very beautifully decorated."

Yes! Laura saw us kissing. Her face was frozen and she was looking at me angrily. She was in shock. I was also in shock. I think the only one who was calm was Luke.

"So, since your mom is here Luke, she can help you."

"No, not Lori. I would like you to help me."

"She better go, Luke. Maybe she needs to cook lunch for her family."

"Mom, Lori is going to finish helping me choose the furniture in the drawing-room. Can you, Lori?"

"I think it's better I go, Luke."

"Okay, Lori, if you need to go. I'll call you later."

"Bye Luke, bye Laura."

I got out of that situation quickly. Laura didn't even look at me. She simply turned her face away.

I got in the car and my hands were shaking. I couldn't even breathe properly, worse, I can't even drive.

I stayed in the car for a few minutes, to calm down. I was very nervous. It felt like I was floating ... What now? Too late!!!

What if Laura says something to Travis? Thankfully, Travis is going to travel and stay a few days out of the country.

Now, at this moment I need to go home. My mother is waiting. Then I will talk to Luke to find out what his mother said.

31 CHAPTER

I got home, parked the car in the garage, and stood there in shock. I could not imagine that Laura or someone I knew could see us together, in a furniture store.

In the middle of my worries, my mother came from inside of the house and asked if we could go to the supermarket.

" Lori! Are you okay? You look pale?"

"Hi mom, I'm fine. Let's go? Will Susan want to come with us?"

"I'll ask again because she didn't answer when I asked her the first time."

Without being able to breathe properly, I didn't feel well. My stomach and head were hurting.

While my mom came into the house asking if Travis's mom would like to go to the supermarket, I ran up to the bathroom and vomited. I was not well. I was extremely nervous. I threw up a few times and sat on the bathroom floor. I was sweating cold and my hands were shaking.

My mom knocked on the bathroom door.

"Lori, are you okay, dear?"

"Hi mom, I'm coming."

I leaned against the bathroom sink and got up. I opened the door and my mother was waiting for me.

"You look like you're sick. How are you?"

"I think I ate something that made me sick. My stomach hurts."

"Lori, lie down for a while. Tomorrow we'll go to the supermarket."

"Can it be, then, mom?"

"Of course! Susan and I are going to cook dinner today. Go to bed."

I went upstairs and saw that my dad and Travis's dad were out enjoying themselves. I closed the door to my room and started to cry. Why am I crying? I think I was afraid of losing Travis ... imagine if Laura tells Travis about Luke and me?

My God! I don't even have words to explain to Travis.

At that moment, Luke texted me.

"Hi, baby! Are you okay?"

I didn't want to answer Luke, but he went on to text me:

"You ran out of the furniture store ... it was because of my mother, wasn't it?

Unfortunately, she saw us kissing, but I denied it. If she asks you anything, just deny it."

When I saw confirmation by Luke's text that Laura saw us kissing, I panicked.

I laid down on the bed ... Do I tell Travis myself, or do I deny Laura what she saw?

I hope Laura doesn't come to my house today. Please, I am hoping she doesn't come here today ...

I didn't even finish thinking. I heard the doorbell ring.

I heard the footsteps of someone coming to open the door. After a few seconds, I heard laughter from my mother, Susan, and Laura! OMG!!!

My mother knocked on the door and called me:

"Lori, your neighbor Laura is looking for you!"

I was silent to pretend like I was sleeping, but my mom knocked on the door again and said:

"Lori, she said that it is very serious and that she needs to talk to you."

"Mom, ask her to come up here, please."

"Sure, I will."

I ran to the bathroom and put foundation on my face to hide my crying.

Laura knocked on the door and I opened it. I've never seen a person with such anger in his eyes, just like Laura's eyes.

I had nothing in my head during the moment my mother warned me about Laura until I opened the door. What excuses would I give Laura?

"Hi Laura, how are you?"

"Hello, Lori! With my stomach sick from seeing you and my son kissing."

"You are wrong Laura we ..."

"Shut up Lori! I'm not an idiot, I saw it! And I came here to give you a first and last warning, stay away from my son!"

"Laura, I think you were wrong. Luke and I are just friends and I went to be nice to him in helping you with his new apartment."

"Lori, when you lie to me, it only makes things worse. I also don't want to know anything about you and my son. I just don't want him to get involved with a married woman. He's very young and there are millions of young, single women out there. "

"Okay Laura, your message was given and I got it."

"If you two continue to meet, I will be the first to speak to your husband and I'm not kidding Lori!"

Laura left looking crazy. But it seems that I

felt relief. At least Laura's intention is not to tell Travis about my affair with Luke, for now.

I went to the bathroom and washed my face. I took a deep breath and went down to be with my parents and in-laws.

Soon after, the children arrived from school and Travis from work. When I saw Travis come into the house, I wondered if he knew about me and Luke. I was desperate, just imagining this situation.

"Baby, are you feeling better? I called here today and my mom said you were lying down. I thought it was weird."

"Oh yes, I got sick in the stomach, but I feel better."

"How nice then!"

32 CHAPTER

Everything was ready for Thanksgiving: table, lunch, drinks ... everything was perfect. Three days of preparation, but everything is finally ready. Travis is very anxious because he is already traveling to Europe tomorrow.

Everyone was extremely excited.

Yesterday, I met Luke for the last time. I went to his apartment and we talked about the situation. We were concerned about his mother.

We made love for the last time, at least, it was for me, but not for Luke.

"Lori, my mother has nothing to do with our life. We are adults."

"Luke, I am married and I cannot do this to my family, to you and myself."

"But I think we love each other, don't we?"

"I think you should be on your way, Luke. What we're doing is wrong."

"Lori, I think I love you. I only think about you, I just want to be with you. Ending our relationship was not in my plans."

"But it is the most certain thing that we can do now. If we continue together it could be worse."

"Lori, any chance that you will end your marriage?"

"Luke, you are much younger than me. This is not appropriate."

"What is it, Lori? We are in the 21st century, for God's sake. This age thing for relationships between men and women, it is already gone ..."

The worst is that I think I'm in love with him. Feeling Luke is so good that it makes me lose the direction of my life.

We put dinner on the table and it was a party. Travis said a prayer, everyone was silent. In that silence, I heard Luke's motorcycle noise. Motorcycle today? I thought, gosh, today is a cold day and he is on a motorcycle. While everyone was praying, I was traveling in my world called "Luke". Just thinking that I won't see him again, my chest tightens.

My desire now was to be with him. I even thought about having a family with him.

Our secret moments will never be forgotten. They are not so secret anymore, but it was my wish.

After prayer, we started dinner. The bell rang, I was shocked. Is it Laura? Or Luke?

Travis offered to answer the door. As I cut the ham for Cody, I heard Luke's voice ... my God, this boy is crazy.

"Luke, come in, just in time! Dinner is on the table."

"Thanks, Travis! I came to bring this apple pie my mom made. And these flowers for Lori.

When I looked into those blue eyes of Luke, with that wide smile, it seemed that my heartbeat faster.

My hands were shaking. So much so that I cut my finger.

"Are you okay, Lori?"

"Yes, Travis. Just cut my finger."

My mom went to get the first aid box while I wrapped my finger around a napkin.

"Can I see your finger?"

Luke asked in front of everyone and I kind of disagreed, but I ended up showing it.

"Wow, the cut was a little deep. Let me help you."

So, Luke took the first aid box from my mother's hand and commented and he took a course in first aid at the Red Cross. My mother looked at me differently and then looked at me very seriously.

Luke and I stayed in the kitchen while my family was in the dining room.

"Lori, I can't stay away from you. Just thinking about the possibility of losing you, I'm going crazy."

Luke was disinfecting my finger and talking about our love. He held my hand with such care. He kissed my finger with the band-aid. At that moment, my mother entered the kitchen.

"Lori, I think you better come over for dinner!"

"Yes, I will mom. Are you coming, Luke, or are you going?"

"I think I better go; my mom is already

crazy, you know ... I left her flowers on the dinner table."

"Thank you, Luke! I'll take you to the door."

Luke said goodbye to everyone and I went to the door with him. I opened the door and he left, turned and said:

"I love you, Lori!"

I smiled at him, but when I realized I saw Laura at her door looking at me and Luke. My God! I forgot the promise I had made to her that I wouldn't meet Luke again.

I went into the house and went straight to dinner. The first person I looked at was Travis, afraid he might have noticed something. But I saw that Travis was involved talking to my father and his. I felt immense relief.

I looked out the window to see if Luke went to his house and saw that Laura was all furious, waving her arms and seemed to be screaming. But, I was so happy because Luke came to see me, which was the only deep feeling I wanted to keep. At that moment, that was it.

"Lori, I just hope what I saw between you and that boy, it was just an impression."

"What's this, mom? This boy is our neighbor."

I turned my face to my mother and started to have dinner. All I could notice were my flowers on the table.

33 CHAPTER

Everyone woke up early and Travis' parents and my parents went to take Travis to the airport. At the last minute, the children asked to go. Good thing there is a big car in this house!

When they left, I took the opportunity to clean the bathrooms very well, the kitchen, and the rooms of the house. A good vacuum will be a great idea!

When I finished the first bathroom, the bell rang. I thought it was strange, it was still early for someone to come here.

I looked out the window and saw that it was Laura. OMG! What does she want with me? It was because of yesterday that Luke came here. That attitude of Luke coming here was not my fault. I think I better talk to her soon before she comes when my parents and in-laws are here.

"Good morning Laura!"

"Lori, I don't think you understand what I told you!"

"Laura, it's not my fault that Luke came here yesterday ..."

"You are a whore, Lori. My son said he doesn't give up on you and I don't accept that kind of relationship! You are a married woman!"

"Laura, Luke and I don't have anything. I don't know why he's saying that."

"No Lori, don't lie to me. I saw you kissing and I already found your underwear in his apartment."

What? I never left anything of mine at Luke's apartment!

Laura came in and we were there in the kitchen fighting. Ridiculous, all of it! my God! And now?

Laura keeps yelling at me. Offending and threatening me.

"Laura, don't worry! I'm not going to see Luke anymore. Now, please, get out of my house."

"Get out of your house, right? You get out

of my son's life, you bitch."

And Laura came at me, punching me in the face. On the first punch, she hit my nose and I felt the blood come out. On the second punch, she hit me in the eye ... what is going on? Then she kicked me in the belly that made me fall.

That was when I didn't even see it. I got up and pushed her away from me.

And that's when she hit her head on the corner of the kitchen island and fell.

After I pushed her, I laid down again because my belly was hurting so much.

I was stopped by the pain when I saw that Laura fell close to the island.

When I looked at her on the floor, I saw that she didn't move and I saw a lot of blood coming out of her head.

"Laura? Laura?"

I got up from the floor and dragged myself until I got close to Laura.

I pulled her over and started calling her again.

I tried to wake Laura and nothing! I got up

and took a piece of paper towel and wiped my bleeding nose.

I took a glass of water and drank while looking at Laura lying on my kitchen floor. "Why didn't you go and enjoy Black Friday, Laura?"

There were no signs of Laura waking up or of the blood stopping.

I took a tablecloth and wrapped it around her head.

When I lifted Laura's head to stop the blood, I realized there was a hole in her head. MY GOD!!! I looked quickly at the corner of the kitchen island and saw that there was blood on it. Where Laura hit her head, there was blood ... and a lot of blood was outside her body that wet the kitchen floor.

I started to despair because as much as I tried to wake Lura, she didn't move ...

"No, no and no!!! Wake up Laura, wake up !!!"

Did I kill this woman?

34 CHAPTER

Laura is very heavy! Carrying Laura from the kitchen to my car in the garage made me very tired.

I called my mom and told her that I would go shopping and that when they got home, I wouldn't be there.

"Lori, Susan, and I want to go with you!"

"Mom, sorry, it won't work, bye!"

I put garbage bags in the trunk of my car and laid Laura down there. Then, I went to clean the kitchen floor and wherever else there was blood. I was shaking a lot!!! Now what?

I'm going to the beach to wait for Laura to wake up. And if she needs to go straight to the hospital? She lost a lot of blood.

Maybe she will need blood ... What if the worst happened? If she died? I don't want to spend the rest of my life in jail. I didn't want to kill this crazy woman!

We went to the beach and stopped the car.

Now, what am I going to do?

The wind is so cold ... the sky is covered with gray clouds. Today, it looks like a funeral day. My head kept thinking about what to do: go to the hospital or wait a little longer?

I opened the door of my car. I walked very slowly to the trunk to see if Laura moved.

I put my finger on Laura's nose to see if she was breathing. No, my God, she's not breathing! I started to cry.

Laura was unconscious and the amount of blood she lost; I think she is dead. She is not breathing.

It seems that my head is empty. I don't know what to do. I can't go to the hospital now, what will be my explanation? Surrender to the police and explain why Laura and I were fighting?

What am I going to do with this body? I'm a murderer!!! I do not know what to do. I stood on the beach for a while, thinking about what to do.

I started the car, took a deep breath, and started driving with no right destination. But I was looking for the right place for me to throw Laura's body.

I don't know where, but I'll find it. I took too long to decide what to do and now knowing that Laura was dead, I needed to resolve this situation.

I am not responsible for all this having happened. Laura came to my house and started to attack me. Now I need to put an end to this.

I drove for about two hours. In the meantime, my mom had called me and Travis and Luke were sending me love texts.

I didn't answer them. Enough, now I must solve this. I started on a path. I thought it would lead to a farm. I saw that there were no cameras on it and I entered my car in the woods. I stopped by a lake.

I got out of my car, walked to the small lake, and saw a good space. Surely, someone would find

Laura's body there, but I wanted her to go away.

I looked to all sides of this place and there was no one. Everything was extremely quiet.

I opened the trunk of my car and started pulling Laura's body. I had to throw her on the floor because I didn't have the strength to hold it. I pulled out the trash bags that were tearing because of her weight.

It took me about thirty minutes to put Laura's body in a ditch. I threw her body there, in the cold morning, and ran out of there. While leaving the road, my car gave the empty gas signal. What the fuck! It was already the second time that the car gave a signal to refuel.

I stopped at a gas station, which was about ten minutes from where I left Laura's body.

I went inside the gas station and went straight to the bathroom. I washed my face and looked at myself in the mirror ... I had no words to describe my despair and relief.

I bought a coffee and went to put gas.

The cold wind bothered me a lot because I did not have a sweatshirt. I was barely able to insert my credit card because my hands were shaking with cold and dread.

"Hey, Lori!"

I heard someone call me. I turned my head and saw that it was Heather, the wife of Travis' boss.

What is this woman doing here?

"Hi Heather, how are you?"

"I am fine, and you? What are you doing around here, Lori?"

What am I doing here? What am I doing here?

Then Heather's dog starts to bark at me.

"Heather, what a lovely puppy! I did not know that you had a puppy."

I tried to change the conversation, avoiding answering Heather about my location.

"Yes, he is really adorable. Russell gave it to me a couple of months ago."

"Wow, I think my kids would love to have a puppy like that!"

"They sure will! Today, our husbands traveled!"

"Yes, I didn't know that Russell was going to travel too."

"Oh yes, he decided last week. It was a last-minute decision."

"So, it was nice seeing you Heather, but I need to go! My parents and in-laws are at home waiting for me to have lunch."

"It's great to see you, Lori. We'll schedule something later."

"Sure, we will. Bye!"

"Bye, Lori!

I left the gas station with my car speeding. I needed to get out of there as quickly as possible.

I got home and everyone was there smiling and having fun. And me, carrying the murderous feeling on my back.

I looked at every corner of the kitchen to see if there was a blood mark there, but everything was clean.

35 CHAPTER

It was the worst night of my life. The smell of blood on my hands did not come out. The pain in my arms from carrying Laura's body still hurt. And outside, the police car lights at Laura's house, burned my eyes.

I got up at five in the morning. I made a coffee and stayed there in the kitchen, remembering what happened the day before. Laura's body was lying there and her blood on the kitchen floor didn't come out of my head.

Everything was dark in my head. I couldn't even think about what I was going to do from now on in my life.

Travis had sent a text message saying that he had already arrived at the hotel in London.

Carrying the weight of killing someone is a tremendous punishment.

Around seven in the morning, someone knocked on the door. It was from Chris, Laura's husband.

"Good morning, Lori!"

"Good morning, Chris!"

"Sorry to come to your house so early, but I would like to know if you saw Laura yesterday?"

"Yesterday? I didn't see her ... Did something happen?"

"Since yesterday, she hasn't come home. She hasn't driven her car and left her cell phone at home."

"Wow, how strange, Chris."

"I called the police last night. They asked some questions, but they will wait for 24 hours to start looking for her."

"I'm sorry, Chris. Can I help you with anything else?"

"No, Laura, I just wanted to know if you saw her."

"Sorry, Chris, but I didn't see Laura."

"Thank you, anyway, Lori, and have a nice day."

"Let me know if you have any news, Chris."

"Okay, I'll let you know."

I closed the door as soon as Chris left. I leaned my head against the door because I couldn't move. I was in shock. My God, now what? I couldn't even cry anymore; I had a lump in my throat.

"Good morning daughter!"

I turned around and it was my mother.

"Good morning mom!"

"Are you okay? Yesterday, you were silent all day."

"I think I'm a tired mom. I think moving to Connecticut, organizing everything, a school for the kids, and now, Thanksgiving! It has all made me extremely tired."

"Calm down daughter, everything will be

fine."

"On top of that, Travis traveled!"

"You could travel with the kids to your mountain home in Colorado. You could spend Christmas there. Maybe you can relax a little bit."

That's right!!! I'm going to our mountain home in Colorado! As I didn't think about it before. I want to stay away from here. In fact, I need to stay away.

"Mom, I loved that idea. It will be great for me and the kids."

"Yes, daughter, it will be great! Travis can travel straight to Colorado when he comes back from Europe."

"We can spend Christmas at the mountain house or with you, right?"

"Of course, you can Lori!"

Immediately, I texted Travis and informed him that I was going to travel to Colorado.

Travis took a long time to answer my message, but that didn't matter to me. I'm going to Colorado anyway.

My cell phone rang. And it was Luke.

"Mom, I'm going outside for some fresh air."

"Okay, I'm going to start preparing lunch."

"I think it's still early for lunch, but it's okay, Mom."

I answered Luke's call.

"Hi, Luke!"

"Hi, Lori! Can we meet at my apartment?"

"Today?"

"Yes, now ... I need to talk."

I was astonished. I wanted to see him, but at the same time, I wondered if he was going to talk about his mother.

And it would make me upset.

But I decided to go.

"Mom, I need to go out, but I'll be back soon."

"It's okay, Lori, but is everything fine?"

"Yes, it's okay, mom."

I got in the car and to my agony, I smelled

blood. My God! What am I going to do with all this?

I arrived at Luke's apartment and we kissed. It seems that I am more in love with him ... or is it just the pity that I killed his mother?

36 CHAPTER

We made love. And it was the best sex I had ever had. We went to bathe together. The water was hot and my body relaxed. It felt like I was quiet around Luke.

Until then, Luke didn't comment on his mother's disappearance.

While we were in the shower, Luke passed his hand over my body, kissed my neck, licked my nipple, and right there, we made love again. He turned me on his back, spread my legs and had oral sex.

My legs were shaking. He sucked me so good that I seemed to be in the clouds. He got up and penetrated me. What a delight to have sex with Luke.

After our shower, we went to the kitchen to prepare a coffee.

"Luke, I'm going to Colorado for a few weeks. I'm going to spend Christmas there."

"Really? Any special event over there?"

"No, I need to see how our house is in the mountains."

"Send someone to check this out for you. I can't be this long without you here with me."

He said that and hugged me. Luke is very affectionate. I love being with him.

"A few weeks will pass soon. You will see."

In that time, my cell did not stop ringing with phone calls and messages.

I went to the sofa and saw that Travis had answered my message and my mother had left me a voicemail.

"Luke, I have to go."

"At least have your coffee, Lori."

"I really need to go!"

"I hope to see you soon."

We kissed and I left.

From the car, I called my mother who was waiting for me to have lunch. I read the message from Travis who did not agree with my going to Colorado, as the Christmas party was already confirmed at Russell's' house.

I didn't answer Travis and went home. Entering the street at home gives me despair remembering what had happened. To make matters worse, a police car was in front of Laura's house. I saw that Chris was heartbroken with no answers about Laura disappearing.

I drove my car into the garage.

I am without action: will I surrender and tell everyone what happened? I will have to talk about my relationship with Luke. I threw her body in the bush. Why didn't I call the police when the accident happened? Everything seems to be against me.

No, I can't say anything. What about my children? Their mother will be in jail ...

I do not know what to do.

I went into the house and my mother had set lunch for me.

"Lori, everyone was hungry. I called you but you didn't answer. They already had lunch, but I separated your lunch."

I looked at lunch and my stomach churned.

"Mom, I'm sorry. I'm not hungry. I'm going to the bedroom for a bit."

"Wait a minute. The police came here asking for you."

"Why?"

"Laura has disappeared and they are asking everyone."

"If they come again, let me know ok?"

I would never have imagined that this could happen to me. I'm a criminal. And I didn't kill because I wanted to, but my actions led me to a crime.

I sat on the bed. Cody came over to say something, but I could barely hear what he was telling me. My thoughts were driving me crazy. My stomach and head hurt.

Travis called me at the time of my torment.

"Hi, Travis!"

"Hi, my love! How are you?"

"I am fine."

"Your voice is not sounding good. Are you sick?"

"I want to go to Colorado Travis."

"Lori, let me come back from England. I don't have the head to decide this now."

"Travis, I think I'm really stressed out. I need a new look."

"Lori, I already booked Christmas at the Russell's' house. I can't cancel it because" my wife is stressed. "

"Okay Travis, ok ... we'll talk later."

I turned off the phone. I was looking out the window and assessing my life.

At that moment, my mother came close to me and hugged me:

"I know you are tired and our visit is getting worse. Thanksgiving and Christmas made you more stressed. But we are leaving next week.

Everything will be back to normal."

"Mom, it's not like that. I love you being here."

"Are you going to Colorado"?

"No mom, I'm not going. Travis had already made a commitment to spend Christmas at his boss's house."

"All right, Lori. Maybe after Christmas, you will spend the New Year there."

"Let's see mom!"

37 CHAPTER

Christmas Party Day

This morning, I already prepared Valerie and Cody's clothes for the party at the Russell's' house. Travis had already chosen his outfit and I had no idea what dress I am going to wear.

Yesterday, I met with Luke. He and his whole family are saddened by the disappearance of his mother.

The police came to my house twice to look for any information.

My agony has taken my sleep and my hunger. I've already lost ten pounds.

Travis thinks I am sick or something. He has no idea what I'm going through.

My light of life has already disappeared with Laura's soul. Because I'm not able to live anymore.

Not because I am thinking about suicide, but I don't see any sense in this life anymore. I wake up in the morning and lie down at night with no goal. I have thought several times about surrendering myself to the police and telling the whole story of that damned day when I became a murderer.

Travis and the kids decorated the house for Christmas.

Travis already scheduled a doctor for me for next week. I don't know if I'm going to see her or not.

"Baby?"

"Yes, Travis."

"Do you need help preparing the salad for today's dinner?"

"Thanks, Travis, but it's ready. I also made cookies to go."

Travis took me by the hand, pulled me up to our room, closed the door:

"Lori, do you need to say something? What's going on with you?"

I sat on the bed, looked at the window, and saw that snow was starting to fall. The snow moved strong and it was beautiful to see that image. How did I love Christmas and snow then? It was a dream to see snow at Christmas.

"Lori?"

"Yes, Travis?"

"Did you hear me, I asked a question, baby?"

What is the use of asking something that I will never answer?

"Travis, I'm tired ..."

"Lori, today we are going to that Christmas party and the day after, tomorrow we are going to Colorado."

Will I improve if I go to Colorado? I do not know anymore.

"It's ok." I answered and went to the bathroom. I looked at myself in the mirror and realized that I had to do something with my hair. I'm looking like a zombie.

"Lori, can I warn the kids about Colorado?"

"I think so, Travis. I think they'll like the news."

I went into the shower to see if the water removed my pain and agony from the moment. The moment that never passes.

I did my hair and a good makeup for tonight.

I decided to put on a black dress to match the color of my soul.

I went down to arrange the salad and cookies to take to dinner.

"Wow Cody, you're dressed really well."

"And me, mom?" Valerie shouted from her room.

"Let me see you, Valerie!"

She came happy with her new dress.

"You look beautiful!"

Valerie and Cody were excited for the party. Soon, Travis came down and we went to the Russell's'.

When we left the garage, we saw that Chris was with Luke talking at the door of their house. The snow kept falling, Travis commented "what a sad time for them."

I couldn't even answer anything for Travis.

"Daddy, do you think the police are going to find Laura?" Cody asked.

"I don't know Cody, but I don't think they will be celebrating Christmas, don't you think, Lori?"

"Probably not, Travis."

"Do we stop by to wish them a Merry Christmas?"

And in that Travis was driving home to Chris.

"Good evening Chris and Luke!"

"Good evening guys."

"Merry Christmas."

"Thanks, Travis, but we are having the worst days of our lives. Sorry I can't celebrate with you."

"We understand Chris, we're sorry."

Then I looked at Luke who looked very sad.

What a situation, my God. That's when Chris came up with something new.

"We are hopeful because the police collected the recorded images of Peter's house and David's house, the day of Laura's disappearance. I think we have clues to what really happened to her."

Peter and David are our neighbors ...

38 CHAPTER

My Christmas party was horrible. My thoughts did not leave the possibility of the police finding any clue as to when Laura came to my house that catastrophic morning.

Thankfully, Cody and Valarie were having fun. There were two other schoolmates to keep them company. Travis, as always, was talking to coworkers. I took a glass of wine and kept pacing trying to avoid conversations.

Russell's' house was just beautiful! The Christmas decoration was super elegant. I think decorating was the only thing that made me a little happy and knowing that life might have some meaning.

The Christmas dinner table was spotless! Everything was in place. The bowls and dishes were perfectly aligned. What a dedication from Heather, Russell's wife.

The fruit table is right in the center of the living room. All the decor was extremely charmful.

After a while, Travis and I talked and I know he knew I was different. Very different.

"Baby, how are you? Are you having fun?"

"Travis, the party is beautiful, but I would like to leave as soon as possible."

"Calm down Lori, after dinner, we can go."

"It's fine then! The kids are having fun, aren't they?"

"Yes, they are! They are growing so fast, aren't they, Lori?"

"Yes, they are..."

"Besides, they are great students and very dedicated. That makes me very happy."

While Travis and I were there talking, Heather approached us.

"How nice to see you having fun! Thank you for accepting the invitation to our Christmas party. Russell was super happy."

"Thanks for inviting us Heather, it's our pleasure," Travis replied.

"Your Christmas decor is spectacular, Heather! Everything is perfect." I added.

"Russell was incredibly pleased with your trip to England. It looks like your project, Travis, will be a success! Congratulations!"

"Yes, I will have to work harder until the end of January and I believe that we will have the financial support that we need."

"Great!" Lori, did you find what you needed that day in Avon? "

"Which day?" I replied as I did not remember that damn moment.

"That we met at the gas station!"

In this, Russell approaches us.

"Are you having fun?"

"Yes, Russell, we are. I thanked Heather for the invitation. Your party is incredible." Travis replied.

"Yes, even our children are having fun, see?" I spoke to see if the conversation changed direction.

"But, Lori, what is even in Avon?" REALLY? Travis asked me that question.

"It was a day that someone commented to me, a mother of Valerie's friend, about Avon's Mall being very good."

"That's true! The Avon Mall is excellent! I bought most of my Christmas decorations there." Heather agreed with me.

Then dinner will be served in 30 minutes." Heather warned.

"So, I'll let the kids know." And get out of there.

I realized that Travis was looking at me differently, but he didn't comment. I pretended that everything was normal. My heart was racing ... I am scared all the time! It is a horrible feeling!

Dinner was served and everything was a success for Heather. Everything is perfect!

My desire was to be far away from there and from everyone. I couldn't smile for a second all night.

After dinner, we went home. Cody and

Valerie fell asleep as soon as they got in the car.

"Lori, I think you should see a psychologist. What do you think?"

"Perhaps."

"You are sad, very sad. And we can see it in your eyes ..."

"Yes, I'm sad..."

"Can I help you with anything, my love?"

"No, Travis, I don't think you can help me. I'm exhausted! I wanted to spend a few days in Colorado."

"Okay, Lori. So, you and the boys are going. I definitely won't be able to go. I need to finish the project proposal."

"Okay! Thanks for agreeing to this trip, Travis!"

"Sure, Lori! I want you good. If you think you should stay there longer, stay as long as necessary. I can stay with the kids."

Through my cell phone, I bought the tickets

to Colorado. The children and I will travel early tomorrow. I felt such great relief. I need to get away from it all.

Early in the morning, I packed my bags and waited for Cody and Valerie to wake up so that I could tell them about the trip.

Travis had a coffee and went to work on December 25.

Too much, for me!

I called my mother saying that we will be early on the 26th in Colorado and if they can pick us up at the airport. Of course, she was super happy to welcome us.

Luke texted me and asked if he could see me.

And we met at his apartment.

When I arrived at Luke's apartment, I saw that the door was open. I thought it was strange, but I entered anyway.

I walked in slowly and saw that Luke was lying on the sofa. He had his eyes closed, he seemed to have cried, his nose was red.

"Hi, Luke?"

"Hi, Lori!"

Luke got up from the sofa, came over to me and hugged me very tight. I noticed he was so fragile. He was surely in agony about his mother's disappearance.

"Lori, thanks for coming. How was your Christmas?"

"It was okay, Luke."

"I bought you a gift."

"You mustn't do that, Luke!"

"Just a little Lori, please accept that!"

I took the gift and opened it. It was a ring with a bracelet, very beautiful ...

"Thank you, Luke! They are beautiful! I loved it. Sorry, I didn't buy you anything. I was so busy ..."

"Lori, I am very upset about my mother's disappearance. This situation is making everyone at home desperate."

When I get close to Luke, I feel relieved about everything ... but how can this happen? How will I deal with this situation?

"Luke, I'm going to be gone for a few days. I'm going to Colorado."

Luke looked at me like I was abandoning him in this difficult situation in his life.

Yes, I am doing this ... I am doing this because I am also in a difficult situation.

When I look at Luke in the eye, I wonder when he will find out his mother's true whereabouts.

My God! Help me...

Luke got up and went to make us a coffee. Too early for wine.

During that moment, Cody sent me a message asking where I was.

I didn't even answer ...

Of course, we made love. It is impossible to be close to Luke and not want his body next to mine.

A mixture of love and sex ... Now, the fear of losing it makes me very insecure.

While we showered, my cell phone rang a couple of times. I thought it was Cody, but it was Travis. When I got out of the shower with Luke, I called Travis.

"Where are you, Lori?"

"I'm on the beach ..." It was the only answer I had to give ...

"Lori, in this cold?"

"Travis, I'm in the car. I'm fading a little. Can I call you back?"

"Calm down Lori! I was just worried. I got home and you weren't there. That's it!"

"I'll be home soon."

I hung up my phone and saw that Luke was watching me, and he was sad ..

"Lori, how long are you going to continue with all this?"

That question from Luke kind of pissed me

off. He doesn't even know that his mother is dead because of our relationship. Precisely because of him.

I'm in this situation because of him.

"I love you, Lori! I want to have a life with you forever. I don't want to be just a lover ... I want to be part of your life."

"Luke, do you know that I have two children? If I separate from Travis, our children would be destroyed.

"I'm ready to accept all of this, Lori. I want to live with you, forever. I love you!"

39 CHAPTER

How wonderful to be in the mountains of Colorado. Breathing the cold of the mountains and the smell of pine trees makes me more alive!

When I arrived, I was cold waiting for the house to heat up from the heater.

Meanwhile, I went to the gas station to buy food and wine for the days that I will spend at our house. How I miss living in Colorado!

I stopped at the gas station and got out. Very cold, but it was bearable. I went down, prepared a very hot coffee for me.

I slowly chose what to buy. What a delight to be able to be there, in

Colorado, alone, and enjoying my moment

of freedom. I bought wine, pasta, and some snacks. I also bought a book to keep me company "Issues", by Paula Avila. From the cover of the book, I know I'm going to love it!

Chocolate powder for my hot chocolate will be perfect! Thank you, God, for that moment. I needed it.

I bought cheese, salami, and ice cream. My days will be full!!! I deserve all this!

Even remembering Luke is delicious!

I think I love this kid, but I don't love the idea of leaving my life to be with him.

Travis is a great husband, and I don't want another husband.

I also bought some magazines.

I went to pay for my purchases.

"Are you preparing for the snowstorm?"

"Snowstorm? What snowstorm?"

"Yes, It will start tomorrow afternoon."

"Is it going to be bad?"

"It is a snowstorm!"

"Well, I think I'll be ready. If the electricity runs out, I have an electric generator."

"So, you're fine, enjoy the storm!"

"How much?"

"The total was $ 78.56."

"I'll pay by credit card."

"Just insert the card, please."

"Okay!"

"Good! You are done! Be safe and have a good day!"

"Thank you!"

I arrived at the house and the first thing I checked was the electric generator...

And there was the generator ... It seems to be alright.

I went home with the groceries.

After I organized my groceries, I went to get wood for my fireplace.

It took me about two hours, but I filled the fireplace with wood and left some for another two days. Well, I think it will be enough for two days.

I opened my bottle of Italian wine and put on a song. My fireplace was in a fire!!!

I cut some pieces of cheese and salami. I sat in the armchair that faced the landscape. Snow landscape ... Too beautiful. In that context, I allowed myself to forget Laura, Travis, and even Luke. I want to enjoy this moment as if it were the last!

And I started to read my book "Issues" ... I drank my wine and I ate cheese and salami ... What a wonderful time!!!

It feels like a dream sitting here, listening to opera, reading a book, and enjoying the snow.

I don't want to reflect on my future today, or even tomorrow. My future is not yet guaranteed or defined. So, I want to live today. Today and now.

The wind outside is getting stronger and the snow is falling more and more.

I woke up scared!!! A lot of wind outside. It was already dark and my fireplace had almost no fire.

I got up remembering the dream ... I dreamed of Laura. It was not a dream; it was actually a nightmare!

I took more wood and put it in the fireplace. It is so cold. I turned on the kitchen light and made hot chocolate. I saw that Travis texted me.

My dream about Laura was that she begged not to die. My stomach hurts when I remember this tragedy.

I certainly won't be able to sleep again.

The wind outside looks like a "horror movie". For a moment, I was afraid that Laura might show up too. My madness!!!

I went to my bag and took medicine to sleep. I don't want to be wandering around the house like a ghost.

I picked up the book and went to bed.

40 CHAPTER

Just like the guy at the gas station said: storm!

How much snow outside. I made coffee and toasted bread.

Being alone is good, but it's a little weird.

I put wood in the fireplace and stood there enjoying the storm and finished reading the book.

Then I called Travis who was fine and working. Travis was super happy with the result of the project and making a dream come true. I texted my mom asking if the kids are doing well, and she said they were fine.

I stayed around waiting for the snowstorm to pass and when that happens

I will clear the entire road for the car to leave.

Travis calls me and I answer.

"Hi love, is everything still going on there?"

"Hi, Travis?

"So, I just finished my project. I finished it faster than I thought."

"That's great! Congratulations!"

"Thank you, Lori. So, I'm going to Colorado, stay with you there at our house."

"Great idea, Travis. But we have a storm over here."

"Yes, I saw it. But I will be leaving tonight and arriving around 11 pm."

"Who will pick you up at the airport?"

"Your father, my dear. I will spend the night with your parents and the children and tomorrow around noon I will try to get around, at the mountain house."

"How nice, Travis. I hope you can get here, there is a lot of snow!"

"I'll try baby, I miss you already!"

"Me too, Travis."

"Then I'll see you tomorrow."

"See you tomorrow Travis."

Being here in Colorado, at our home, makes me feel a little happy. Being here made me miss Travis. Miss our old life…

Around seven in the evening, it stopped snowing. I went outside and the snow hit my knee. But it was cute. I remembered that we have a cart to clear the snow. Lucky that I brought gasoline to the electricity generator, I put it in the snow cart and started making it work.

I tried several times and nothing. I went into the house and made a hot chocolate to warm up, it is very cold outside.

I took advantage and put more wood in my fireplace.

I went back to the garage and tried to start the snow car. One, two and the third time the cart worked. I felt relieved.

It took me a long time to clean the driveway and the entrance to the house.

In the middle of the cleaning, I saw a deer family ... how beautiful it is to see nature. They kept looking at me and wandered through the forest.

I went into the house and went straight to the bath. I put hot water in the bathtub, and I also put on a very relaxing song. I added some salts and soap in the water and I got into that "magic hot bathtub". Wow, how relaxing was the water.

I laid my head on a towel and traveled back in time remembering when I, Travis, and the kids, were young, and we came here every weekend, at the mountain house. Great moments…

I could do anything, but the feeling of guilt towards Laura, don't leave my head for even a second.

In this moment of agony and thoughts, Luke calls on my cell phone.

"Hello, Lori!"

"Hello, Luke."

"How is your vacation?"

"It could be better, but I'm resting."

"You are alone?"

"Yes, I am. Today there was a snowstorm, but now everything is normal."

"Should the landscape be beautiful?"

"Oh, yes, this is magnificent!"

"Lori, can I spend a few days there with you?"

"Luke, I would love to, but Travis will be back tomorrow."

"Really? What a pity! I miss you."

"Do you have any news from your mother, Luke?"

"No, Lori, nothing yet. We are in distress without size. My father is devastated."

"I'm sorry, Luke!"

"Thank you, Lori. It would be better if you were here with me. I love you, Lori!"

"I need to go, Luke."

"Okay, I hope to see you soon."

"Yes, we will see each other soon."

41 CHAPTER

One more night alone. It is exceptionally good to enjoy moments of reflection. Especially when we are alone. Thoughts fly into the past, bringing good memories, making life worthwhile. But when we return to the present, nothing cures it if you made a mistake or missed something important in your life. At that point in my life, I made a mistake and lost all my history. Years of history that I build alone and with my family. So much has changed and could change for the worse.

To think that my own decisions made me get here. If I had been more aware of my actions and not been so selfish, everything could be different.

But I know I will have to act when I get back to Connecticut. I know I will not be able to live with this guilt inside my chest. Waking up every day with the weight of being a murderer is not in my plans. The shame I will give Travis, my parents, and the children. I will not be able to erase this from their lives. I, alone with my terrible actions, destroyed the lives of people I love the most.

I got out of the bath and put on my robe. I looked out the window and saw only the white snow on the pines. Beautiful view!

I went to the kitchen and made soup. The fireplace was almost without fire.

I had to go to the garage to get more wood to put in the fireplace. I went with my robe. Wow, very cold!!!

I grabbed it well so that my arms could hug it. I put more wood in the fireplace and went to finish my soup. I cut bread and served myself. What delicious soup. I could not describe how good it was having soup in the cold. Especially being able to enjoy the view of the snow outside.

Travis texted me that he had arrived at my parents' houses and that everyone was fine. I returned a message saying that I was also fine and that the snow was clear around the house.

The fireplace even lit up in the kitchen. What beautiful colors the fire produces ... They could enchant anyone ...

Travis continued to send messages, but the

most important thing was to say that he will arrive here on the mountain tomorrow around noon.

It was a good surprise that Travis was coming. It will be good for him to relax a little. I began washing dishes when my phone rang. Strange, I looked and it was Luke.

"Hello!"

"Hello, Lori?"

"Hi Luke, it's me. How are you?"

"You won't believe it. I just landed in Colorado!"

"What do you mean Luke?"

"I just arrived in your land. I wanted to see Colorado."

"You are kidding with me?"

"No, I'm not. I'm going to get a uber taxi and I'm going to your mountain."

"Luke, Travis is going to be here tomorrow ... no, no way."

"I'm just going to spend the night with you and I'm leaving early tomorrow."

"You are crazy, Luke!"

"I really am, Lori! I'm crazy about you!"

I laughed ... I thought I'm going to enjoy this crazy love ... I sent the address to him. And I said I would pick him up at the gas station.

I got the car and went to get him. When I got there, I didn't get out of the car so the guy at the gas station wouldn't recognize me.

I saw that the guy kept looking at my car all the time, but I stayed right there. After about thirty minutes, I saw that Luke arrived. When I saw him, my heart rejoiced ... but Luke went into the gas station ... oh no ...

Immediately I texted Luke saying that I was already waiting for him outside.

I saw that he went to the bathroom and then went to buy some snacks.

Luke talked to the gas station guy and left. He saw me in the car, gave me that beautiful smile that only he knows how to give and came. I realized the guy at the gas station was looking in Luke's direction until he got in my car.

"Hi, my beautiful!"

"Hi, Luke! How was the trip?"

"It was excellent! Just to see you here, so beautiful, everything is worth it!"

We gave a super passionate kiss and went to the mountain house.

When I got there, I heated the soup for him and prepared him a bath. Luke was delighted with the house and nature there. The snow on the trees made everything more beautiful, even at night, it was brighter.

Right there in the kitchen, we started kissing. He seemed to be crazy about me. He kissed me and caressed my whole body. What a wonderful man!

Luke knows how to drive a woman crazy ... I don't even know why he's in love with me. He could have any woman on his feet.

And right there in the middle of the kitchen, we made love! It was so good that I couldn't even feel guilty. My life lately is one mistake after another. Being with Luke is my best sin.

After our delicious love, we got in the bath together. He opened a bottle of wine that he had bought at the gas station.

"Wow, Lori! Being here with you is a gift. I'm having a hard time. It's not just me, but my whole family."

"I can understand Luke. I'm sorry for you all."

"Lori, drop everything and come with me!"

"Luke, please ..."

"I received a job offer in California. We can move there. Cody and Valerie, at first they might be surprised, but then they would accept me. "

"Luke, I can't promise anything for now. I need to work things out first ... nothing is easy for me now. So that kind of decision won't happen."

"So, you don't love me enough to leave Travis, am I right?"

"It has nothing to do with Travis, it's me Luke."

Luke and I stayed up all night talking and telling me his dreams. I think all the men I get involved in, love to work and have a million projects.

Around five in the morning, I took Luke to a hotel in the neighboring city.

"Please Lori, think about my proposal. I know it won't be easy. But think about you and your future and know that I love you."

"Okay, Luke, I'll think."

"Promise?"

"Yes, I promise."

I drove back home on the mountain. The scenery on the road was perfect and remembering Luke's smile made my soul happy. But there is no chance that I am going to live with him ... even if I divorce Travis, I don't want anyone around.

I got home and went straight to bed to sleep. I know Travis has arrived around noon, but I need to sleep.

42 CHAPTER

I woke up to a noise at the door, probably Travis. I looked out the window and saw that the day was cloudy and it made me want to sleep more.

As I dozed off, I realized that Travis came into the room, gave me a kiss, and closed the curtains. I lifted my head:

"Hi, Travis!"

"Hi, baby! Keep sleeping, I'll go outside and take a look at the house ok?"

"OK."

I closed my eyes and slept. I slept so much that I almost woke up at night.

I could smell it coming from the kitchen. I realized that I was starving. I got a little dizzy and went to see Travis.

"Hi Travis, I'm sorry that I slept that much."

"It is okay, Lori. I'm making soup for dinner."

"It smells really good. I'm hungry."

"It's ready in a little while. Do you want to have a wine with me, baby?"

"In a little while, Travis. Everything's fine with the house, isn't it?"

"Yes. After the winter is over, someone will have to come here and take a look at the central air conditioning."

"What about the children at mother's house?"

"They were fine. Cody was at Corey's, his friend from school."

"Oh yes, Ann and John's son."

"Yes, yes."

I looked out the window and saw that a little snow was still falling. The pines were heavy with snow.

"Lori, it is so nice to be here today. It reminded me of when we bought this house. Cody and Valerie weren't even born. Do you remember?"

"Of course, I remember Travis. We were super happy. It was in the spring and it was still cold at that time."

"We could come with the kids this spring and go on the river, go fishing and build a fire outside ..."

"Of course, it would be great for us and them."

I started setting the table for our dinner while Travis poured wine for me.

Travis came with the wine glass and kissed me. I know he wanted to prolong the kiss, but I took the cup and went to put more wood in the fireplace.

"I miss you, Lori."

I didn't answer Travis. I took a sip, and the wine was particularly good.

"Travis, the wine is perfect!"

"I bought it at the liquor store near your parents' house."

"Very good."

"Baby, can you cut the bread for us, please?"

"Sure!"

"The soup is almost ready, a few more minutes and that's it!"

"This soup smells delicious, my God, I'm so hungry!" I commented.

Travis started to open a drawer here and there. He seemed to be looking for something.

"Baby, do you know if we have candles around here? I wanted to put them on the table."

"Ah, try to look in the closet in the dining room. I think the last time I saw it, if I remember correctly, was in there."

"Yes! I found two, they are used but it's fine."

Travis placed and lit the candles on the table. He put the soup in a tureen and served it. I had already cut the bread and put it on the table too. Travis put on a song and asked me to dance. Why not. Let's enjoy the moment.

"Lori, I know you were very lonely and took care of the move to Connecticut practically alone. Then you took care of the children and me all the time. I want you to know that after my project is over, I will be with you more and I will help you more, at home."

I only heard Travis' words. Yes, I was alone in CT, but not so alone.

My future is not so certain yet. Everything can change when I get back to Connecticut. So, I will enjoy it now, today, because tomorrow does not belong to me.

We sat at the table. Travis and I kept talking and laughing. That's when I realized how far I and Travis were apart after we moved to Connecticut.

I know Travis was focused on making his project happen, but it cost a little.

My involvement with Luke has no explanation, but it existed in my life. And from my involvement with Luke, it brought me a reality that I will have to face. The accident with Laura had no reason to happen, but it did. And now everything can change.

"Hey, honey, did you like the soup?"

"Travis, this is delicious."

43 CHAPTER

After dinner, Travis and I sat on the couch in front of the fireplace. We put a blanket on us and laid there together. But we stayed there in silence for a long time. Travis and I seemed to have secrets, and at that moment we seemed to be reflecting on those secrets. I don't know Travis, but I have a very complicated secret.

The silence was still there, but I just wanted to enjoy the fire in the fireplace, which was magnificent.

My cell beeped. I got up to see who it was. It was my mother, asking about the New Year. She wanted to know if we were going to dinner at her house or not.

"Travis, the New Year's party will be tomorrow. Will we go?"

"You know love."

"I didn't want to, but your parents will be there and if we don't going, it will be sad, isn't it?"

"Alright, Lori. Our trip to Connecticut will be on the 2nd, right."

"Yes, did you book on the same day as ours?"

"Yes, I did."

"We better go to celebrate with our parents and children."

"So, I'll let you know that we'll be there tomorrow around 4 pm."

"Perfect! Come on, Lori, lie here with me?"

"I'm going, I'm going."

I went back to Travis' arms and slept.

Early the next day, Travis and I organized the house.

I threw away some old things, while Travis took a look at the basement and garage.

Travis locked the house and we left for my mom's. While driving, I stopped and took a look at that beautiful view that was of our mountain home.

Snow still decorated the pines and the afternoon sun made everything more beautiful.

We arrived at my mother's house around 4 pm. I went straight to the kitchen to see if my mom needed help.

Cody came and gave me a hug. I asked him where Valerie was and my mother from the kitchen replied:

"Valerie went to Travis' mother's house. They will arrive at 7 pm for dinner."

"Mom, do you need help?"

"Hi Lori, how was the house?"

"Hi mom, the house was great. I thought the house needed more care, but everything was working."

"What a great daughter."

"So, mom, can I help you?"

"If you want to place the crystal glasses on the table, it would be great. You need to wash them ok?"

"It's ok."

I stayed around helping my mother and Travis

went to take a shower.

Then he went to the kitchen and stayed around helping with some things. My father soon arrived from the mall.

Later, I went to get dressed for dinner. I put on a white dress. I fixed my hair and applied a stronger color lipstick.

Around 6:30 pm, everyone arrived. Valerie, Travis' parents and Travis' older sister.

It was a party. After a long time, I managed to have a little fun. It seems that my heart was lighter. For a while, Laura's image didn't come to my head.

We had dinner and the food was delicious. Travis's mom brought baked fish.

My mother made pork, pasta, and salad.

Right after dinner, I stayed around helping with the dishwasher and excused myself and went to bed. Everyone was scared because I went to bed before the New Year (we always watched together to see the ball fall in New York, on television), but today it wasn't like that.

As soon as I entered the room, Travis came after

me:

"Baby, are you okay?"

"Yes, Travis, I am. I'm just tired and want to enjoy my last few moments of rest before we go back to Connecticut."

"Okay, really rest. I love you."

Wow, Travis saying he loves me, it was a while that he didn't say that phrase.

I put on my pajamas, turned off the light, and closed my eyes, and slept.

44 CHAPTER

I opened my eyes and it was still early. It was time to get up because my alarm went off.

Another day of struggle and accepting my reality. The reality of shame and pain.

I hardly slept all night. Thoughts came and went. Memories of my childhood, marriage, children, husband, and even Luke.

The road of life changes with such speed and direction, that in a blink of an eye, everything can change. The only thing we can do is accept it.

I got up and went to brush my teeth. I fixed my hair and put on makeup.

Not a smile could come out of my mouth.

I started to hear noise coming from all directions. People were waking up.

Today we are going to work outside.

I lost many pounds and the urge to eat doesn't even exist anymore.

I've always tried to look at the positive side of things. But for the past six months, nothing makes sense.

I may even feel that I am paying for my actions, but the price is very high.

I talked to Travis yesterday and he is satisfied with his project. He was accepted by the college and financed 100 percent by the University of London. Everything is going according to plan.

I was medicated with antidepressants and they have helped me a lot.

I am working six hours a day in a factory. A tedious experience, but at least it helps to pass the time.

Today, I'm going to have tea and eat a piece of bread.

I'm going to start early on my job today.

During the commute to work, I remembered the last trip I went to Colorado. We always have great times at the mountain house. Wonderful moments with my family.

My work is about 45 minutes away.

Today was hot, and at work, there is not much ventilation. Summer ... I wanted to be on the beach. Cody and Valerie went to Colorado. They must be having a lot of summer fun over there.

There is traffic early in the morning, especially when I return from work. Also, I have nothing to do. Sitting in traffic is no longer a problem for me.

After an hour in traffic, we got to work. I don't know how a person is capable of working in this very repetitive field. Starting at the University of art, my mind needs to be open, see open landscapes, see the color of nature.

Today at 4 PM my lawyer will visit me. I am very anxious about the news that he will bring me. I guess that's why I didn't sleep well.

How great it was to go to college. It was certainly one of the best experiences I had in life. Being young, knowing and facing the unknown is magical. Everything in this phase of life is fascinating. I met Travis in college. He was super smart. He was the best in class. He graduated with merit. Travis always dreamed of changing the world. He wanted to find a cure for cancer.

Much of Travis' research and studies have been approved in many laboratories.

The staff stopped for a snack. I sat there in the corner alone and ate a cereal bar. Today, not everyone wanted to participate. I think the heat is a bit irritating. For the first time, I wanted to leave soon. I need to know my attorney's news.

45 CHAPTER

When I arrived from work, I went to the restroom anxiously.

After the shower, I was waiting for my lawyer, who arrived promptly at 4 pm.

"Good afternoon, Lori!"

"Good afternoon, Dr. William."

"Are you all right, Lori? You are thinner than the other time I saw you."

"Dr. William, I have no desire to eat. My life is, you know, destroyed."

"I know Lori, I know. But today, unfortunately, I don't have good news."

"Please, do not say that."

At that moment, it seemed that my world had collapsed and without a positive sign of the law, I feel as if it is better to die.

"Dr. William, I can't do it anymore, I'm doing my best, but it's difficult."

"Lori, I understand you, but in these cases, you need to be patient. The judge says that you need to be in jail for another six months. After that, you can appeal again."

"My God, six more months ..."

"I'm already filing a new request to make your time more flexible. Ending six months at home."

"How likely is this appeal to be accepted?"

"Almost zero chance of the judge accepting, but Travis wants to keep trying."

"Well, do what needs to be done, Dr. Williams. I am incredibly grateful."

"Lori, behave well here, work hard and be patient. It all counts in your favor."

"Thanks."

"Have a good night, Lori."

After talking to my lawyer, I went to dinner. A soup that only had water.

My life turned into hell. Psychologically, I tortured myself every day to make up for being here. Physically, I tortured myself because I don't eat. I don't forgive myself.

After dinner I went to my cell. My orange outfit is the only color in this place.

Everything here is dark, even people's souls are dark.

I lay down and thought about the possibility of getting involved in that place.

Maybe I can talk to someone in the jail and offer a painting course for inmates. Painting has always been my joy.

Eleven o'clock at night. I still couldn't sleep and tomorrow at five in the morning, I will get up for work.

"Did your lawyer bring you good news?"

Teresa, my cellmate, asked me.

"No, he didn't."

"Christmas here isn't that bad. At least the food is less bad."

When Teresa said "Christmas", I cried. My body writhed in pain. I realized how much my life has changed. And how much I changed people's lives. I remembered when Chris cried in court when he said he missed his wife at Christmas, and that I, at the time, knowing the truth, had not said anything.

46 CHAPTER

BACK FROM COLORADO TO CONNECTICUT

Early in the morning, Travis and I woke up and organized our bags. I went to wake up Valerie and Cody. My mom went to make us a coffee so we could catch the plane.

"It was great of you to stay here with the kids."

"Thank you, mom, it was great to spend these days here. I was in need."

"Come on, it's time."

My father came to call us to give us a ride to the airport.

Hugs happened and we went to the airport. From there, we said goodbye to my father, who needs to go to work and we entered the airport.

While we checked in, my heart was so small and full of agony. I knew that arriving in Connecticut, I was going to have to take action on Laura's death.

"Lori, are you ok?"

"Travis, when we get home, we need to talk."

"Of course, we can. But is there anything I can help you with?"

"No, Travis, there isn't. I want to talk at home because I don't want to talk around the children."

"Okay then."

During the drive back to Connecticut, it reminded me of the first time we came. At that time, we were super anxious and happy and today, everything has changed. It changed because I made a mistake and changed the course of my story, my family's story too.

The plane landed and we walked to our car that was in the long-term parking lot.

The children were already tired and tomorrow, they have school.

When we get home, I will make dinner for them.

I realized that Travis was worried about me, but he soon understood my distress.

I'm surprised that Luke didn't text me once after we met at the mountain house in Colorado. I wonder why?

And when I got home, I did everything my way, started dinner and did the laundry.

The kids stayed in their rooms organizing things for school and Travis snuck into the office.

The bell rang and I went to the door to see who it was.

"Good afternoon, Mrs. Anderson?"

I saw that it was the police and my heart ached.

"Good afternoon. How can I help?"

"We are here to find out about the disappearance of Mrs. Laura, your neighbor at the front."

"Yes, I know her. I can help."

"We need you to accompany us to the police station. '

"Now? I am preparing for dinner."

"Yes, now."

I called for Travis who came a little scared.

"What's up?"

"I need to go to the police station."

"Why?"

I got close to Travis, kissed him, and said in his ear:

"I'm going to need a lawyer."

Travis was in shock and stood there while I went out with the cops.

"Travis, turn off the stove or finish making dinner."

As I headed towards the police car, I saw that Chris and Luke were at their door. I lowered my head and kept walking, got in the car, and saw that they were still looking at me. Luke hugged his father, who seemed to be crying.

My God, what have I done?

Arriving at the police station, I entered a small room, where an investigator turned on a television and started showing me a video.

And in that video, it contained the image of Laura going to my house the day she died. After playing the video, Laura went to my house and never left. It only showed my car leaving and returning later.

"Mrs. Lori, as you can see in the video, Mrs. Laura never left your home."

I didn't answer anything and the investigator continued.

"You know why you're here, don't you?"

It was then that everything came to my head again: me pushing Laura, who was beating me. And she accidentally fell on the corner on the kitchen island. And she died. How horrible to remember that? But, that moment, there with the investigator, I needed to tell the truth, because the truth was there in the video

After that day, I never came home again. From there, I was already arrested.

Travis hired some of the best lawyers to

defend my case.

But I never told him about Luke. I think it would be too much for Travis. He would suffer too much, and have no reason for me to have caused

Laura's death. It left everyone dumbfounded. Only Luke knows the truth.

To this day, Travis asks me what really happened, but I just confirm that it was a stupid argument, between Laura and me, and that ended in this tragedy.

I never wanted to kill Laura, never, God knows that. But life surprises us so much that we become accidental killers.

For everyone, my attitude toward planning the whereabouts of Laura's body was the worst.

Nobody can understand, if it was an accident, I could have called someone or even the police, but I didn't do that. I killed and hid the body.

47 CHAPTER

After a few months of being in jail, Luke came to visit me. He brought me some snacks and a rose.

When I heard that he was out for a visit, I was helpless and ashamed of him seeing me in that situation. But I decided to talk to him.

I entered the room and I saw him, sitting there, waiting for me. I almost cried. He reminded me of wonderful moments I spent with him. But it's because of him that I am here. A foolish passion changed the direction of my life completely.

"Hi, Lori! '

"Hello, Luke."

"Lori, I brought you these things. I had more but they did not allow me to bring it."

I took the bag and looked inside. I looked at a KitKat and it made me want to eat.

"Thank you, Luke."

We looked at each other for about two minutes. We could not get words out of our mouths. But that silence spoke so much, that if we said anything, it would all be a lie.

"Lori, are you okay around here?"

"Luke, look around you and answer that question."

"Sorry, Lori, I know this sucks. I just want to know if" you "are getting all this?"

"Luke, you know why I'm here, don't you?"

"I think so, at least I know why my mother and you are at odds."

"Our disagreement was about our relationship."

"Lori, but you didn't have to kill her. '

"Fuck you, Luke! I didn't kill your mother; it was an accident. A stupid accident."

And I cried. I cried at that moment because of all my anguish. Because for the first time, I was able to vent the truth to someone.

"Lori, I love you and I'm sorry that this happened to you."

I looked at Luke who looked at me with pity and love, and it seems that his eyes made me feel peaceful. I can't explain, but he looked at me with love without blaming or judging me. And at that moment I needed support and no more looks of guilt.

"Okay, Luke. Thanks for coming over here."

"I want to hug you now, Lori."

"Luke, please don't come here anymore. I don't want to see you anymore."

"Okay, Lori."

When I said this to Luke, it looked like he was relieved. And he just got up and left the room. He didn't even look back.

Funny how life changes direction. And our life changes so often that there is no time to think or plan anything. It only changes, without you authorizing it.

48 CHAPTER

The jail administration authorized me to teach inmates a painting course.

They said that I will have a location and that we will have two classes a week. They asked for my graduation diploma.

After six months in jail, I felt hopeful. I don't know why I was hopeful, but I was satisfied.

I called Travis and told him where my diploma was and asked him to send it to me. I told him that I will teach painting in jail and he was surprised.

One morning, after breakfast, the jail manager called me.

"Good morning, Lori."

"Good morning, Mrs. Smith."

"I have your diploma and I would like to talk more about the painting course. I already have a room and I would like to take you there to see what you will need."

"Of course."

We left there and went to a super dark room. We went in and I immediately said that we needed more lights there.

"How many people will I give the course to?" I asked.

"How many people can take the course, you tell me."

"We can start with twelve people, because this room is not that big."

"Then make a list of what will be needed for this course that I need to make a budget and ask the State for money."

That was when Mrs. Smith left and the police officer who accompanied us took me to the van to take me to work.

This feeling of being a teacher, made me feel a little better as a human being. At least, I can offer something to someone.

After I arrived from work, I took a shower and had dinner. When I returned to my cell, I started planning the painting class. I made a minimum list of what I would need to teach the class.

All this planning made me satisfied with myself. After finishing the shopping list, I handed it over to a police officer who was around.

Life in jail is not easy, a lot of rivalry between inmates. Drugs, sex and violence is normal.

I never thought there was such a life. I will never talk about what happens inside this jail. It is better to live there in silence and when you leave here, try to forget everything, absolutely everything.

In order for me to get my entire list and start my class, I had to have a romance with Mrs. Smith.

Living in jail is so humiliating that everything that happens inside is accepted.

For fear and security, let's say I dated this woman. Yes, we made love and she was very kind to me. I never thought about being with a woman but being with her was one of the best parts of my days in this place.

My class will start tomorrow. I am super anxious. Many inmates want to take a painting course, but we don't have enough space. Each course will have a duration of two months and then we will start another one. After I started having a romance with Smith, everyone in jail respected me, even the officers.

Smith sent me good luck yellow roses for my new stage inside the jail. I was happy to receive the roses. They are so beautiful.

49 CHAPTER

I dreamed about my children all night. How much they miss me and how I miss them much more. The routine of getting up early and preparing their breakfast was wonderful. I miss my life so much. Taking care of my home and my family was everything to me. And I threw it all out on a whim. My own whim.

I woke up missing my children, but for them, I am starting a new project today inside this jail.

Within a small hope arises that I am a better human being.

After my breakfast, I went straight to the classroom. Everything was organized, the canvases were in place, and more lights gave a particularly good look too.

The inmates started to enter the room and I

realized that they were also anxious but happy at the same time. Maybe a new light at the end of the tunnel for them. After they all sat down and looked around at the brushes, canvases, and paints, they were smiling at each other. Two policemen stayed inside the room and to my surprise, Smith came to congratulate us for the effort of perhaps a new career.

"Thank you, Mrs. Smith for the words." I said, looking into her eyes. My look was one of gratitude, and her look at me was one of love.

"Good morning, everyone. Thank you for participating in the painting class. It will be very important to have patience and strength too. Do not give up on this journey. I am here to give my best in the knowledge received by my teachers. And I hope you enjoy it. "

"Teacher, why are you in prison?" A detainee in the corner of the class asked.

"I would like that here, in this small painting class, that we only talk about art. We will not bring our past here. But after the class, I can tell you the reason that brought me here."

And I started to give the first ideas about painting, how to use brushes and use paints. Everyone wanted to draw something, so let's go. I said that each one could draw a tree, the sky and maybe a lake.

Let the imagination work, but don't worry about the quality of the design, because we will work on that during the course.

And so they started to paint. Some were laughing, showing it to colleagues. It was great to see people smiling and happy. Forgetting who they really are.

It was a good feeling on the first day of painting class.

"Girls, girls the class is at an end. See you in the next painting class. Thank you!"

And so they went out and talked to each other. The woman who asked me why I was in jail, stopped in front of me.

"So, teacher, you can tell me now."

I finished fixing some brushes that were out of place and wondered if it was convenient to say why I was in jail.

At this point, Smith entered the class and asked this detainee to leave.

"How was the first day of class Lori?"

"Much better than I planned. Everyone was engaged. I hope they stay that way."

"This afternoon, go to my office. Let's celebrate your success with a good wine."

"Okay, Smith, I'll be there."

After everyone left, I started vacuuming and mopping the classroom. I removed the garbage and put clean bags in the dumps.

The room is ready for the next painting class.

50 CHAPTER

The jail gates opened and there they were: Cody, Valerie, and Travis. My mom and dad were here in Connecticut, but I asked them not to come.

What a hug I was able to give my children. I embraced with love, pure love, without charge.

While hugging my children, I looked at Travis who looked at us with tenderness and love.

After pouring out my infinite love to my children, I hugged Travis. I hugged him with love, but it was a more friendly hug.

Travis was instrumental in my parole. Without his insistence, I would still be in jail.

I looked back before getting in the car. I never wanted to remember the existence of this place in my life, but I know that it will be impossible. Everything that I went through inside, I will never forget.

I also changed a lot as a person. I am no longer a lady of society.

Everything changed in my status.

Valerie and Cody were talking to their father, and I no longer felt part of their life. It was eleven months away from their daily life, but it seemed that the distance was a lifetime. Valerie had her first period and I was not there.

Cody had a little girlfriend who I didn't even know. He told her that his mother was out of the country studying. I was ashamed to tell her the truth.

Travis moved to Branford. Woodbridge held no hope for him and the children at school.

I looked at Travis who took pity in me and started a conversation.

"Lori, we are so happy with your return home."

"I missed you so much."

The children were silent.

"Lori, your mother is preparing for Christmas and is cooking her favorite dishes."

"Thanks Travis. I want to thank you for all your support and apologize for everything."

"Lori, let's start our life over again. Everything that has happened, we will forget.

Travis showed me pictures of the new home in Branford. A beautiful and very comfortable house. It was close to the beach.

The kids at first didn't want to move, but after my case was on TV, they were embarrassed and agreed to move.

While Tavis was driving home, I enjoyed the sea. It felt like I was out of the water. It seemed that I didn't belong in that life.

I took a deep breath. Travis held my hand and said calmly.

"It will not be easy, but we will need time for everything to return to normal."

"Thanks, Travis, for the support. I will always be grateful."

Travis parked his car in the new house and I

soon saw my mom and dad coming towards me.

My mother came crying and incredibly happy, but her face showed pity for me. My father just hugged me.

I entered that beautiful, clean house. Everything was very well decorated and clear. What a satisfaction it was to be there.

I only brought some personal documents from the jail, but nothing else. I just wanted to take shower and change clothes.

I saw a beautiful Christmas tree. Everything was decorated and lit up.

Christmas music made everything calmer and more peaceful.

I went straight to the bathroom and took a shower.

Now, I was happy to be here with my family but at the same time was afraid and insecure of beginning life again. Carrying a crime on your back and having been convicted is awfully bad. A feeling of not belonging to society and knowing that your children are sick of you, hurts even more.

Everything gets heavier.

My mom had prepared a bathtub with salts for me. I think Travis actually guided her.

That bathroom was all white and clean. The marble in the sink gave the impression that I was in the sky. The perception of being able to have a hot tub seemed to have been rewarded.

The perfume of salts with rose petals in the bathtub water seemed to be a dream.

The water was hot when I got in. Delicious. I laid my body down and finally felt a little comfort after a long time.

I have scars on my body that are unexplainable, but I can never forget them. These scars will never fail to show who I once was and what I did.

I laid in that wonderful water for minutes with my eyes closed. I was able to travel throughout my life. Despite everything, I could breathe and not cry.

Being positive will not be enough. I must deal with restarting life because it will never be the same.

BOOKS BY AUTHOR PAULA AVILA:

These are my books and I, personally, would like to invite you to read them.

Feel free to contact me at:
paulamgavila@gmail.com
Phone number: (203) 676-3899
https://www.instagram.com/AuthorPaulaAvila/

Book illustrated by Elizabeth Smolinski
www.elizabethsmolinskigallery.com